Arthur Lewis

The Master of Riverswood

Vol. II

Arthur Lewis

The Master of Riverswood
Vol. II

ISBN/EAN: 9783337052140

Printed in Europe, USA, Canada, Australia, Japan

Cover: Foto ©Andreas Hilbeck / pixelio.de

More available books at **www.hansebooks.com**

MASTER OF RIVERSWOOD.

A Novel.

BY

MRS. ARTHUR LEWIS.

IN THREE VOLUMES.
VOL. II.

London:

SAMUEL TINSLEY,
10, SOUTHAMPTON STREET, STRAND.
1876.

THE MASTER OF RIVERSWOOD.

CHAPTER I.

WHEN a man marries a pretty, a graceful, and a sufficiently amiable woman, he is, as a rule, too much enamoured of her, for the first year or two, to find out whether he is really a disappointed man or not.

For instance : William — we will say — remembers well how his Georgiana hung upon his accents when he gave her the abstract of that magnificent speech of Lord Thunderbolt's (the subject of which inter-- ested him so deeply at the time) ; and how, on another occasion, when he made some remarks on the subject of fossils, and asked her if she was interested in geology, she had replied that "she was very fond of it; and thought no study more interesting," etc.; he remembers too, with what rapt admiration she gazed on the starry skies, when he led her out on the balcony on the night of Mrs. Crushemup's ball. A month after marriage, he finds that she does not know the name of the Prime Minister; two months after, he discovers accidentally that she does not know what he means by "strata": and shortly afterwards he becomes aware that she does not know a star from a planet, and is confused as to her ideas of the equator, and the geographical position of Greenland. She asks "who was Professor de Morgan?" and she "fancies she has once heard the name of Professor Tyndall."

However, she confesses her ignorance in the most winning manner possible; she lauds her dear William's cleverness, and "is quite sure there never was any one so clever, or with such a memory as he has," and dear William forgives the innocent deceit she has practised on him, and does not know,

after all, if he cares that she should understand scientific books, 'or want to hear the
leading articles. He would perhaps get
fewer praises, and be less wonderful in her
eyes, if she did. And then time proves
that Georgiana is a first rate cutter-out of
little frocks, has a capital taste in baby
sashes and ribbons; and directs her cook
to perfection. And is William a disappointed man after all ? Far from it.

Again : Maria has always believed that
dear Edwin's taste for poetry was something quite uncommon, and indeed absorb-
ing. He informs her that "he adores
Byron," that he has an excessive admiration
for Mrs. Browning, Tennyson, and Long-
fellow ; in fact, "thinks them all perfectly
divine." After marriage, she finds that
Edwin can fall sweetly asleep in the midst
of the most exquisite parts of the " Lotus-
eaters," or has been quite absent in mind,
" thinking of that confounded fellow Robinson, my love," who owes him that hundred
pounds, all the time she has been reading
the songs of the Eden Spirits in the " Drama

1—2

of Exile ;" or sending poor " Hiawatha " on
his fearful forest-search for food !

This is, of course, terrible. If Edwin
cannot do the repentant gracefully, and
with tact ; if he omits to say that he is a
savage and a brute, and that, as sure as she
is a sweet little woman, he will be a better
fellow] next time, it is all up with him ;
as far as any lingering belief in his sentiment goes.

" It was that beer which did it all,
Maria. Where did you get that beer ?" For
the future, he will take a little Marsala or
Sauterne at dinner. Thinks it will suit
him better. And the fire's so awfully
large, or it's so confoundedly hot : "who
made up that fire ?"—or "why don't you get
outside blinds to this room, my love ?" And
she shall give him a cup of strong tea, and
then go on about the " Lotus Eaters," and
really mustn't she confess, there is something
very soporific about Mr. Tennyson's metres ?

This is all very well. But as time goes
on, Maria finds that dear Edwin always falls
asleep when he is read aloud to, and seems

as if he couldn't possibly help it. This is a great blow. There are some tears, and a certain ideal image of Edwin, which Maria had kept faithfully by her during all the time of their betrothal is finally broken up for good, and seen no more. But there comes a little Edwin, to occupy mamma's attention, and then a miniature Maria, and then Tom ; and then the darling twins ; and so on,—and is Maria either a disappointed or an unhappy woman ? Not at all ; and she never opens Mrs. Browning from one year's end to the other.

We have been supposing cases where the little illusions formed during courtship break up with but slight sense of pain, if any ; vanish without leaving any blank that is not speedily and efficiently filled up. But it is not always so. Sometimes the awakening is sudden, sometimes very slow ; but there *are* awakenings whose bitterness is as the bitterness of death ; whose surrounding shadows whelm and stifle the soul, whose retaliation upon every by-gone dream of happiness, every clinging fancy,

or loving hope, is as that of an avenging
fiend.

And yet, we do not speak of any such
awakening as this. There is still another
kind, a gradual, almost unconscious realiza-
tion of facts that had been kept obstinately
out of view, while the day-dreamer dreamed
on at his will, lying " deliciously" among
the flowers of his own fancy, all planted,
and tended, and watered, by his own hand.
At last, but very slowly, dawns the morning,
when " the dreamer dreams no more."
There is no sudden shock, no sudden fading
of every flower at once, no great wrench of
every tendril from about his feet, his heart ;
he hardly knows when or how they first
began to leave him, but they are all, or
nearly all, gone at last. He may not suffer
vitally or very painfully, but he suffers ;
and God only knows when, and how, that
unknown and un-confessed suffering pains
him most !

The first winter after Rochefort's marriage was one of almost constant visiting,

or of entertaining company at home, of receiving calls and returning them; all which vanities, combined with the necessity for dressing which they entailed, exactly suited Mrs. Rochefort's tastes and inclinations. At this time she and her husband were very happy on the whole; he, because she was so much admired, and always looked so beautiful and still more because she was often so prettily affectionate towards himself; and she, because she was made so much of, and had such lovely rooms, and such perfect carriages, and because all her dresses were such an entire success as to fit and style. In the spring they were to have gone to town, but Nora caught a severe cold about the middle of April, and was forbidden by the doctor to think of wearing low dresses for some months to come, so the going to town had to be given up. It was a dreadful disappointment to her; but Rochefort would have been thankful for the reprieve had it not been for anxiety about her evidently insecure health. A warm summer, however, and half the

autumn at the sea-side, appeared completely
to restore her to her usual strength, and
winter found her more blooming, and, if
possible, more lovely than ever, with the
hope of London in the coming spring
looming like an ever-bright horizon before
her.

"You see I was right, mother, in taking
her to St. Lawrence and Dover, instead of
Brighton," Rochefort would say, fondly regarding his pretty wife as she sat holding a
velvet-and-pearl-and-bead-decorated screen,
between herself and the fire ; while he, with
splashed boots, and gaiters, and spurs, fresh
from a ride of twenty miles or so, sat in un-
congenial proximity to a marvellous "Louis
Seize" cabinet, all ebony, and gilding, and
exquisitely coloured "Watteau pictures."

(What with velvet-pile carpet, high pier
glasses, cut glass "fonts" for moss and
flowers, old China, and new French cabinets,
the "great" drawing-room at Riverswood
was a transformed, and a very splendid
apartment.)

"Yes, I know you detest Brighton," Mrs.

Longley remarked on one occasion, "now *I* detest Ramsgate."

"It's jolly out of the season, mamma," returned her son, "and the boating was the making of Nora. She used to row."

"You oughtn't to have let her then."

"Oh, nonsense, mother. It did her a great deal of good. And it was more fun, knowing nobody. And there were such jolly little fellows in the same house; three little sailors, with long, fair curls, and blue and white check suits, and yellow boots, all as brown as berries, and enjoying themselves as if they were in Paradise. I bought them all boats, and twice took them out rowing. I wouldn't have missed seeing them go out in the morning with their boats or their spades in their hands, and their hair waving in that glorious sun and sea-wind, for anything you could have given me."

"You are very fond of children, Rochefort," was his mother's remark, in a sort of half-asleep tone. Rochefort suppressed a sigh, then began whistling, and walked to the window, where he looked out upon darkness for some five minutes, and never spoke.

His wife went to the piano, and played to amuse herself. She had not noticed his sigh ; for, in fact, she had been thinking of something else, and she was not anxious to have children yet. She was more than contented as things were ; she would even have half rebelled at first against anything that had lessened her absolute freedom to enjoy herself as she would—more than all, that would have raised a barrier between her and her anticipations of crowning hap- piness—crowning success—in this wonder- ful coming season (her first) in London.

That she had very little love of the country, or of a country life, her husband discovered before they had been married six months. She always stopped him in what she called his "stupid farm talk," before a dozen words were out of his mouth : sometimes by moving to the piano and playing a waltz ; sometimes by setting out the backgammon board (she was very fond of backgammon), and sometimes by kissing him ; but stop him she always did. As the spring and summer wore on, Mr. Longley found she had no interest in the garden either, and hardly knew, or cared to know, the name of one flower from another ; that she did not take the least interest in the dairy or the ferneries, or the green-houses, or the poultry-yard ; in the poor people, or the servants, or his model cottages, or his new machines, or his crops, or the schools, or in fact, in anything.

She professed, indeed, to be rather fond of horses, and she was very fond of driving, and drove a great deal about the country (when she could get Mrs. Longley, one of her sisters, or her husband to ac-company her) in a pretty little low carriage with a pair of perfectly white ponies. She was not "fast," and she was too lady-like to be a flirt ; but she was never so happy as when she found herself either the best dressed woman, with the most be-witching hat, and the most faultless gloves and whip, at a meet of the hounds, or the centre of half a dozen admirers in her

drawing-room, as she stood on her fleecy
wool hearth-rug after dinner, her sparkling
fan in her pretty restless hands, a falling
mass of silk and lace tumbling about the
masculine boots for a yard behind her,
and knowing as well as she knew her
name, that the trembling diamond cross on
her breast was being the temporary adora-
tion of more pair of eyes than (in the
carelessness of her conscious power) she
would have cared to count.

It happened one day, shortly before the
time came for the London visit that Mrs.
Rochefort was awakened rather suddenly,
to a sense of how far this delightful and
unclouded state of existence was, from
fulfilling her husband's ideas of strict duty
in this present life, and on his especial do-
main.—The awakening came after this wise.

A man who had been employed for the
past year or so as a carter on the home-
farm at Riverswood, courted and deceived
a pretty young housemaid in service at the
Hall ; an orphan, and a girl of only two-
and-twenty.   The elder Mrs. Longley was

at last informed of the circumstances, and that the girl was in great distress and wished to leave, but had no friends to whom she dared to turn. Mrs. Longley told Rochefort. Rochefort had been fastening on his gaiters in the room where he kept his guns, powder-horns, whips, boots, and what not, and she came to him there. His horse was waiting for him at the back-hall-door.

"I suppose you'll send the man off the place, shall not you?" said his mother, when she had finished her story.

"Off the place?" repeated Rochefort—turning on her a look she never forgot; and then without more words he went out. Instead of going the road he had intended, however, he struck off down a narrow lane, and in about ten minutes was at the gate of a field where several men were engaged in barley sowing.

"Is Robert Elliot on the field?" asked the master, with a stern face, as Gray came up to him, touching his hat.

"Yes, sir; he is with the drill."

" Call him to me, and take on the drill yourself."

The bailiff walked up the field, and sent the man down to where Rochefort still sat on his horse, that uncommon look on his face more settled there than before.

The man touched his hat.

" Are you Robert Elliot ?" asked the master.

" Yes, sir."

" Have you been courting a young woman at my house called Elizabeth Neale ?"

The man looked down—twisted his hat uneasily in his hand—coloured, and then became pale.

" I have come here to be answered, sir," said Mr. Longley.

" Well, sir," hesitated the fellow, " there has been something of that sort."

" She is going to leave—do you know what for ?"

No answer.

" Do you know what for ?" repeated the master, raising his voice a little. His horse swerved as he spoke, and he quieted it with his hand; but his blood was boiling.

Probably the man would have lied if he had kept his eyes lowered; as it was he raised them for a moment, and caught sight of the expression in the eyes above his. Then he saw that lying would come too late. He muttered a few words of cowardly excuse for himself and then of cowardly hope "that the master wouldn't be hard on him this time."

"Are you going to marry her?" was all Rochefort's reply to his confused confession and dastardly self-justification.

"Well, I don't know as I can do that, sir, to tell you the truth."

"You can't?"

"I've been engaged this two or three years, sir, to a young woman, a cousin of mine, that'll have a bit of money when her father dies. She's given me her word, and I've given her mine; and it 'ud be the ruin of me to break it off. All the same, sir, I'm very sorry all this has come about, and I hope you'll look over it, sir, this time."

Rochefort waited a minute, till he could command his voice and his temper sufficiently to speak. His impulse was to take the man by the throat, and shake him like a dog.

" "Are you scoundrel enough," he asked, " to mean what you have just said to me? What right have you to come after any woman at my house, and ruin her, and leave her to her ruin? Can you answer me that?"

"Well, sir," said the man, half turning away as he spoke, "it's my own affair, sir, after all, as I see. The girl was soft on me herself, and——"

"You damned brute!" exclaimed Rochefort, roused to such passion that he hardly knew what he did. He raised his hunting whip, and struck the man heavily across the face. The other turned with an oath. The master sprang from his horse, grappled with him, threw him, and beat him, till his whip was broken into fragments. Then, flinging the pieces away from him, he mounted his horse in a fever from passion and exertion, and rode off the field. Gray, who had come on to the scene of action a minute or two before, because he thought the man was being murdered, opened the gate for him, Rochefort's means of opening it for himself being gone.

" See that that fellow walks off the place at once, and never comes near it again," was all he said.

Gray went back to the blubbering rascal, who was swearing he would be revenged on "that young devil, and have him up for assault if he lived another hour."

" Try it on," said the bailiff, with cool contempt, when he had heard his story ; " find the lawyer who will take out a summons against him. Now, you've heard my orders—you had better be off."

The master rode home, and took lunch with the ladies. He never spoke to them during the meal, and followed them into their morning-room when it was over.

" Have either of you seen Lizzie, or spoken to her ?" asked he, standing on the rug, stern and flushed. She had been in the house about two years, and it was her only home.

No; neither of them had.

"When did you know about all this, mother?"

"A day or two ago, Rochefort; but I knew you would be so angry about it, I hardly had the courage to tell you."

"Did you know of it, Nora?"

"Yes, Arthur" (rather timidly).

"Which of you is going to speak to her, and ask where she is going when she leaves here?"

Silence. The question was repeated.

"I really don't see that it is any business of ours," remarked his mother at length.

"Whose business is it, then?" demanded Longley.

No one volunteered the information.

"The girl has no mother; and she has been with us a long time, and worked well, Mrs. Robinson says. It is utter nonsense to say that it is no business of ours," continued the master.

"Well, Rochefort, you can do as you

like, and what you like," retorted his mother, rising from her chair; "but it is time we dressed to go out. The ponies are ordered for half-past two, and we have a call to pay. And you must not forget you dine at the Bishop's this evening, and he is very punctual."

Nora, who was a very obedient and tractable daughter-in-law, rose from her chair at once.

"Stop!" exclaimed her husband, in a voice that made them both turn and look at him. "The ponies can wait—I cannot."

"You cannot, Rochefort?" repeated his mother.

"No. God knows I have waited long and patiently enough to see the end of all this."

"Of all what, Rochefort—what do you mean?" asked his wife, reddening a little.

"Of all this living, and acting, and thinking only for oneself. When is one to begin living for anything else?"

"I never understand you, Rochefort, when you get into this strain," returned

2—2

his mother, reseating herself, and taking up a screen, with a yellow fringe of half a foot deep, which she waved up and down before her face in some agitation; "and I think you say a great deal that is both ungentlemanly and unkind when you become excited."

"And I am sure it is very untrue that we live only for ourselves," pouted Mrs. Rochefort. "We give away lots of money in charities every year, and all the servants are paid regularly, and are well fed, and seem very comfortable; and I am sure, when I feel ever so lazy and tired, and only fit to sit by the fire, or lie on the sofa, I exert myself to return our calls, and be civil and friendly to people. I don't very well see what we can do more, in our position."

Her husband looked at her while she uttered these words with an expression quite impossible to describe.

"Are we doing our duty by all our servants at this moment, Nora?" he asked, after a minute's silence.

" Well, really, Arthur, I cannot see, any
more than mamma, what we are to do.
The girl has behaved very wrongly, and of
course, though it's very sad, she must suffer
for it. It would not do to appear to
encourage this sort of thing by too much
indulgence."

" ' Too much indulgence !' " repeated her
husband ; " don't talk such utter rubbish !
What do you think I want you to do ?—
Only to find out, as any other woman
would, what is to be done with the girl —
and where she is going—or ought to go."

" Thank you, Rochefort, for saying ' as
any other woman would do,' " returned his
wife, much offended.

" That is all you think about—that I
blame you," continued her husband in great
excitement ; " you do not consider for a
moment whether I am right in blaming
you. Are any of us right ? Have any of
us been leading the life that we ought to
do ? In Christ's name, *how long* are we to
go on living only for selfish pleasure, and
following every fancy, with the world sin-

ning and suffering round us every day—
and all day long?"   He began to walk up
and down the room, while the ladies sat
quite silent, in some dread of what would
come next.   "This is only an instance,"
pursued Rochefort, "of the way we are
going on, careless of everything but our
own comfort and convenience.   I don't
know, of course, whether anything could
have been done to prevent this—this affair;
I suppose not.   I hold no one to blame
but the brute himself.   But now that the
evil is facing us—at our doors—it is our
duty—*your* duty, as women, to see what
can be done for her, and not to rest either
till you do it."

"I can call on Lady Harriet Debenham,"
said his mother, "if you like.   She knows
all about those great London institutions,
or hospitals, or whatever they are; and I
dare say we can do something for the girl,
as you are so determined about it.   But
she's got an aunt, somewhere—why doesn't
she go to her?"

"God bless Lady Harriet!" pronounced

Rochefort with some emphasis; "she is always in some good work. She is a true woman!"

Lady Harriet Debenham was a woman of about thirty, and the daughter of the then Dean of Gowerford. Before Rochefort was married, he and she had skated together, danced together, sat side by side at dinner-parties, talked together by the half hour, believed in each other to the back-bone, and, apparently, in all but age, suited each other to a T. Yet Rochefort had never loved her for a moment; and she had only loved him for about half an hour, once in her life; and that was when she sprained her ancle on the ice, and he got her on to a sledge-chair, and then helped her brother to carry her home on it, and, finally, went for the doctor, saying that "Gowerford was only half a mile out of his road in going home." Lady Harriet had been married about three years ago, to a man nearly twenty years older than herself, and with his liver affected, but with a pretty property. She had two or three children, but she still gave herself up, as she had done for years before her marriage, to good works and words of every kind. She was an extreme Ritualist, and had an oratory in her dressing-room. But in spite of her Ritualism (or by virtue of it), she was a good and a " brave " lady.

" God bless Lady Harriet !" Rochefort had said ; " she is a true woman."

" You had better go to her yourself, then," said his wife, rising with some dignity (she was not deficient in spirit of a sort, when once roused) ; " she will perhaps do more for you than for us."

" I shall not try her," responded her husband, briefly.

" I should not be so shy myself of asking favours from a person I thought so *very* highly of, and who was so entirely capable of granting them," retorted Nora, who was considerably flushed.

" I had rather ask the favour of my wife, and let her be the one to do what is right and just," said Rochefort, in a low voice that was intended only for her.

Nora did not speak.

" And now, mother, will you just see this poor girl before you go to Lady Harriet ?" demanded Mr. Longley after a pause.

" If you so decidedly wish it, Rochefort. But I have a great objection ; and you may depend on it, Elizabeth would rather see me at Jericho. I shall do no good."

" This is what it has come to, then," said her son, with bitter emphasis ; " I thought it had. What else can any of us expect ?" And he walked suddenly out of the room.

" How very unkindly Rochefort has spoken !" began Nora, as soon as the door was shut. " I never would have believed he could be so violent and unjust."

" You don't know Rochefort, my dear, as I know him," responded the elder lady, uttering the words, it must be said, with a certain tone of satisfaction ; " I never believed that you did know much of each other before you were married ; you know I didn't. However, you must go through what other people have to go through, and learn to know each other now." And then they went and dressed for their drive.

That night Longley was on his knees before his pretty wife, asking her to forgive him, if he had said anything unkind ; and watching for her returning smiles with eyes in which tenderness and anxiety were equally mingled. And when they kissed each other again, the old ténderness, the old throbbing love and hope of his heart, came back in its passionate, though now weakened and passing power, and made him believe himself for a few moments almost as blessed as he had once hoped to be.

CHAPTER II.

"SIDNEY, listen here," said Mr. Ernest Glanville one morning, as he leaned over the table in his brother's sitting-room, studying the ' Times.' 'Mrs. Rochefort Longley, by the Countess of Hallingford." By George, then, they're up in town, and she's been presented. I wonder where they are. Why hasn't Arthur written to me ?"

" There are some cards for you, I think, on the mantel-piece," returned Sidney, slightly moving his head in that direction, " you had better look at them."

" Oh," remarked his brother, after having opened two or three; " ' 13, Eden St., May-fair :' Thursday. That's the style. I shall be glad to see that young man again."

" To say nothing of the lady," put in Mr. Glanville, who was going on with his paper.

" As you observe—to say nothing of the lady. Well, I must say good-night to you, Sid, and go and dress. It's nearly ten o'clock, and my lady will be down-stairs in ten minutes."

Ernest called the next day in Eden Street, and found Mrs. Rochefort at home. She was too entirely delighted to see him to disguise her pleasure, and he stayed half-an-hour, forcing himself away when he did go. Her beauty, her exquisite toilette, and her pretty animation during the time he stayed, fascinated him. The next day he met Rochefort at their club.

" Do you know," said he, " that your wife will be the beauty of the season ? What has come to her ? She is simply perfect."

" Is she prettier than she used to be ?" asked Longley. ·

" Prettier ? She was a plump, bonny little girl enough—lovely, if you like—but she is a beautiful woman now, with five times the expression she had. And she will improve, of course. She will be fascinating à rendre fou, before the season's out."

" My wife ?"

" Yes, your wife. I see you don't appreciate her," said Ernest, laughing, "I shall have to give you some lessons."

Dissipation was still to Nora a winged and blooming cherub ; it had not become a painted and crippled hag. On the gilded wings of this cherub flew by week after week of incessant and—as it seemed to her —constantly changing pleasure. All the days, and as much of the nights as her husband would give her—were consumed by balls, dinners, ' at homes,' flower-shows, garden-parties, water-parties, drives—God knows what. The vain, the pretty, and the extravagant little woman was in Paradise. To please her, Rochefort condemned himself to this life till the middle of July. Then he became resolute, and she was obliged to go home with him.

It was time :—her bloom was faded, her

spirits variable ; her appetite nearly gone, and she had long ago been driven to all sorts of " pearl powders" and " rose powders," to keep up appearances.   Only her husband and her maid, from whom there could be no concealment, knew how she looked when she laid her weary little head on her befrilled and embroidered pillow at two, or three, or four o'clock on those lovely summer mornings. When they were back at Riverswood, her husband almost swore that she should never go through a season again.

" Really not, Arthur ?" demanded his wife, in considerable alarm.

" No, it is killing you."

" But if I am a very good girl, and get quite strong and well ?   I shall be all right after we have been to Scotland, and to the sea," pleaded Nora.   " It was only the late hours."

" Why are you so very anxious about it?" he asked, looking at her with some uneasiness.

She gave him an answer that was not

the true one, and almost reproached herself the next moment for doing so ; but
it satisfied him, and she considered that was
all that was wanted. She told him that
when she was in the country she was miserable, because she had given him no children.
In London she had too much else to think
of, to think about it.

Nora took great pains to be what she
called " good " during that autumn and
winter. She wished her husband to be
satisfied with her, that he might indulge
her. Besides, she was not without heart,
though she had never known what it was
to be in any sympathy with him, and
though most of what heart she had was
given elsewhere. She felt that she owed
him something—(that is, a show of affection
beyond what she really had for him—she
had a great deal of *gratitude* for the position he had placed her in) for the disappointment which it was impossible he
should not feel deeply, and the results of
which in the future were likely to be serious
enough. Riverswood, for the first time

since the Longleys had had possession of the soil, would go out of the family, if she had no child.

It is difficult, or rather impossible, for a woman to play a part the year through, however, without making a serious trip at some time.   Nora was sufficiently womanly and sufficiently attached to her husband to be really anxious not to "fail him" at every point.   She saw perfectly well that she failed him at a great many, and knew that she would continue to do so; but she had sense enough to perceive the utility of holding certain cords that opened certain doors in his heart in her own hand and she would have given them up to no one. He was not made for her, but he was her husband; he had been her lover; he had opened the world to her; he was almost recklessly generous in his expenditure for her; she was grateful to him, and she perhaps loved him as much as it was possible for her to love a man of whom she was sure, and whose life no longer seemed to consist in the acts of admiring her, and in following her about wherever she went.

This being the state of things, it was unfortunate that one day, not long before the time fixed on for the second visit to town, Nora, by some obstinate preference of her own, as opposed to some very decided wish on the part of her husband, contrived to irritate him beyond (for the moment) his power of self-mastery. He spoke with almost bitter vehemence to her (it was the first time he had ever done it, and as usual in such cases, it was with the repressed feeling of months, and with more vigour than the case demanded) about the want of interest she showed, and had always showed, in everything that most deeply and truly interested and concerned him.

" You are no help to me," he had said at last. " I love you—love you passionately ; but I feel you do not love me, or you would not for ever damp and chill everything that is best in me. Everything that is most longing for utterance in my heart you keep down ; you do not understand me if I speak to you, you think me strange, fitful, fanciful ; and I—I would almost die for you to love me with your whole full heart. Why do not you do it ?"

As she looked at him in almost terrified amazement, he gave a sudden deep sob, and drew her to his breast. She was frightened into saying something soothing to him ; what, she hardly knew ; but she had, at any rate, the tact not to retort on him for the words he had just spoken. She was both moved and unnerved at the sight of his (to her) inexplicable distress.

" There Rochefort, don't ! It is dreadful to me to see you like this. . . . Yes, I do love you, I do, indeed ; how can you ask me ? Indeed, I do not mean to disappoint you."

At the end of ten minutes, such is the strange infatuation of a man's love, he was almost happy again—was holding her on his knee, and pressing her shining hair to his lips, and telling her to forget what he had said : he had not meant it !

But after he had left her, Nora set herself to recall his words, to ponder over them, and gradually to grow indignant over them.

What right had he to speak to her like that? What right had he to *feel* so towards her? In what way did she not do her duty by him? "She chilled everything that was best in him!" She had not even a conception of what he meant. It was very wicked to speak so. Had she ever prevented him reading, or going to church, or doing anything right that he wished? Had he not plenty of friends to talk to, when he wanted to talk on subjects that were beyond her? Mr. Rutherford, and then the Bishop, and Colonel Saville, and that Gray, and—yes, and Lady Harriet Debenham; but then Nora did not quite approve of the friendship with Lady Harriet. If he wanted to marry a clever woman who could talk about religion, and politics, and sentiment, and Shakespeare, and goodness knows what, why, for goodness sake, hadn't he married Lady Harriet, and she (Nora) could have married some one who would have appreciated her more.

Other men did not seem to think her so deficient or so unsympathetic. She was happy enough in society, and every one got on with her, and she got on with every one. It was most particularly unfortunate that she should have married a man who was not satisfied with her, and who wanted her to be all sorts of things that she could not be.

Nora began after this to make rather a virtue of being amiable towards her husband, and of not retaliating on him (" by little things that she could have said on her side if she had wished ") for the unpremeditated and excited speech she could not bring herself to forget. She never told her husband she remembered it ; but she never saw him without the words being more or less recalled to her mind. Her vanity was wounded, and her vanity was one of her tenderest points.

.. They were to go to town again at the end of April. One afternoon, as Gray was superintending the sowing of a field of clover, he saw the master approaching, over the furrowed earth. He came up to them, and looked on for several minutes. Gray noticed that his face wore the expression it had often worn lately ; a sunless, and almost stern expression ; yet the words he spoke were only indifferent.

" You will be leaving off work directly, sha'n't you ?" he asked, after he had stood and watched the men for a little time. .

" Yes, sir ; we shall be leaving the field in ten minutes."

" It's good seed," said Rochefort, taking a handful out of the sack, and then throwing it carelessly back again.

" I believe it is, sir."

The master stood for some minutes more, watching the sowing, and slightly whistling as he did so. Suddenly he said,

" I should like to see the spring-wheat field before I go. It's hardly out of your road home ; you can come with me now ;" and the two moved off the field together.

" Finished the barley ?" inquired Mr. Longley, presently, as they walked along.

" Sown all I am going to do this year, sir."

" Oh, and I want to see the young calves,

at your place, don't forget.   We can cross
the fields to the house."

After they had left the spring-wheat field,
the bailiff asked,

" Are you going up to town this summer,
sir ?"

" Yes ; didn't I tell you so ?   In three or
four days."

" I shall be glad to see you back, sir.
The place doesn't seem itself without you."

Rochefort made no answer, but walked
on.   All at once, however, he said, abruptly,

" Gray—you know who is the next heir
to this estate, don't you ?   My heir, I mean,
in case anything happened to me ?"

Gray felt as if his heart for a moment
stopped beating.   He stood still on the
road, and looked at the master.

" Your heir, sir ?"

" Yes," returned Mr. Longley, laughing,
" but I don't mean that I feel symptoms of
typhus fever, or galloping consumption, or
that I'm going to throw myself over the
next bridge.   You needn't look so appalled,
my poor fellow."

Gray drew a sigh of relief.

"I am glad to hear you say so, sir. I didn't know what you meant. I know nothing about your heir, sir. . Who is he?"

"My only cousin, the son of my father's sister, the Earl of Hallingford."

"And are you friends, sir?"

"We have never been friends, Gray, and never shall be. He is a dissolute blackguard."

The bailiff walked on in silence.

"This man may be your master any day."

"Not *mine*, sir," answered Gray, bluntly.

"Yes, *yours*," said Rochefort; and, as he spoke, he turned a steady look on the man, a look that was never forgotten. "Let me feel that you, at least, will be faithful to the old place; be faithful to it for me, Gray."

The bailiff could not answer a word.

"Mr. Longley," he said presently, with some effort; "do you believe that anything is going to happen to you?"

"No, not at all. I am not superstitious, or nervous either. But, of course, one cannot mount a horse without the chance of

being thrown and killed ; one cannot go a
railway journey without the probability of
being smashed ; one cannot, in fact, live for
an hour without risking one's life in some
way or other. That's all I mean. I may
die any day, and then, all that's entailed of
this estate goes to my heir—a fellow who
is sending all that he has to the devil
already."

"There ought to be a lot of justice in
heaven, sir, I often think," replied his bailiff,
"to mend all the injustice and random
ordering o' things we seem to have here."

"I suppose there is no random ordering
of things, in fact," replied the master after
a minute's silence, " though the look out's
often dark enough to us. But what a happy
fellow you are, Gray," he continued, suddenly turning his face on the man. " I wish
I were you. You have no need to complain
of the ordering of things, as you call it.
Heaven has been very merciful to you," he
added, with a tinge almost of bitterness in
his tone.

"I was not thinking of myself, sir," answered the bailiff. "God knows I have cause enough to be grateful for the change there has been in *my* life."

They were at the farm then, and nothing more was said. The master gave ten minutes to the consideration of the young stock, and five to that of some repairs that were wanted, and then remarked—

"You've never shown me your child, Gray. I should like to see it. Can I come in now ?"

"My wife would be very proud and pleased if you did sir. This way. Maggie, the master has come to see the little one, have you got him there ?"

They entered the low square kitchen, with its fire brightly blazing ; the table laid ready for tea, everything in perfect order, but no mistress there yet. Rochefort leant for a minute against Maggie's ironing table before the window, and looked round him. He knew the room well ; and had known it ever since he was a little fellow, and used to beg his nurse to take him there, to see the china shepherd and shepherdess on the mantel-piece ; and to be given oven-cake to eat.

There was a great oaken dresser, dark with age and polishing, against the wall, and bright and various crockery that was never moved except to be dusted, or upon great occasions—such as a christening, a marriage, or a burial—ranged upon the shelves. From multitudinous nails depended shining jugs of every size and shape ; from the time-honoured brown stone jug downwards ; and on the slab beneath stood old Davison's desk, and old Mrs. Davison's work-box, and the family Bibles of both families, and various other treasures, each on its own mat. In the corner cupboard, which had its door fastened back, were arranged all Maggie's treasures in the way of china and glass, her few little wedding presents, and her mother's old tea caddy, and four silver spoons. The walls were hung with coloured prints, and " samplers " in frames : it was, altogether, a comfortable, warm, home-like looking place, and Rochefort was in no hurry to leave it when he had once entered.

He had a natural love of simple, patriarchal farm life, in no way lessened by his constitutional pride, and reserve of character, or his entirely autocratic sense of his own power and position.

("He has the strangest mixture of qualities," his agent, Mr. Forrest, once said of him, "that I ever saw in mortal man.")

"Maggie, are you coming down?" Gray called at last from the bottom of the stairs. Yes, she was coming this moment; she had only been up to make father comfortable, and take him his tea.

"What's the matter with old Davison?" inquired Rochefort.

"He's had a bad cold, sir, that's all, and Meg made him stay in bed a day or two. He will be out and about when he's down stairs. However, here's the baby, sir, if you care to see it."

"Here—where?"

"In this cradle, sir."

The master took his hands suddenly out of his pockets, and moved away from the ironing table against which he had been standing. He saw that Gray was gently lifting a shawl from the head of a great, dark oak cradle on rockers—the cradle in which Maggie and four brothers and sisters had all been rocked by the mother who would now rock no more.

Rochefort seated himself on a chair near the little bed, and leaned forward—his arms resting on his knees—the better to see the sleeping baby face beneath.

It was that of a fair, healthy, bonny child of four months. The little thing's dark thick hair clung in close tendrils to the head; the dimpled hands and arms, and a part of the little fat neck, lay bare, the coverlid being thrown off almost to the waist. The baby's frock and pinafore were tied up on the shoulders with ribbons, and round its neck was the narrow blue cord that held its rattle. The little breath came soft and regular, the deep sleep was dreamless and calm.

The master sat and watched, as if he had eyes for nothing but that innocent face, ears for nothing but the gently coming breath. Maggie came down the stairs, but her husband put his hand upon her arm, and motioned to her to keep quiet. They both stood still near the door, and looked, but never spoke. Presently, they saw a firm, white, rounded hand, with a glittering diamond on it, move gradually towards the child's head, and touch—as if it touched a sacred thing—some of the tumbled curls above the little brow ; then the old attitude was resumed, resumed and kept—till it almost seemed as if the watcher had been struck in the position he so motionlessly retained. At last, Gray went up gently, and stood beside him. The long and abso- lute silence had become oppressive, almost painful ; and the man broke it by saying,—

" He's a bonny lad, sir, isn't he ?"

Rochefort rose.

" He's a bonny lad—yes," he repeated, evidently making an effort to say even that; " but I must be going now. Good-bye, Mrs. Gray ; I'm afraid I shall not see any of you again for some time."

*　　*　　*　　*

Not far from the house —under the shade

of his plantation trees — which, in that
hour,—with all other things belonging to
him—appeared so worthless, he flung himself down, and hid his face against the chill
ground.

"And this is how God blesses the poor!
. . . . . . Oh, my God, my God !
What have I. done, that I should be shut
out of the only Eden left to me on earth ?
—the Eden of possessing a little child, to
call me father !"

The next morning, as Maggie with her
maid was at work in her dairy, she heard
a horse's hoofs rapidly approaching the
house; they stopped at the gate; it was
opened, then swung too ; and looking up,
she saw the master standing in the door-
way, whip in hand, and booted and spurred
for riding.

" I hadn't time last night," he said, " to
see your father.   Poor old fellow, he would
feel it, if I went without saying good-bye
to him.   Is he upstairs ?"

"Well, he is, just now, sir ; but he's

coming down as soon as ever I've time to see to him," answered the busy Maggie.

"It's all right," said the master; "I haven't more than ten minutes to stay," and he bolted up the narrow stair-case, four steps at a time. Maggie heard them talk cheerfully together, for nearly half an hour; the talk being varied once or twice by bursts of Rochefort's rich, pleasant laughter.

It was the last time the old servant and the young master ever met in this world: but they will meet one day, let us hope, in that kingdom which is reserved for all "faithful servants,"—whether they be faithful in small things or in great.

Just before mounting his horse, Mr. Longley said—

"By-the-by, Maggie, I want to leave this with you, as a plaything for the child." He took from round his neck a silver chain, with a little jewelled dog-whistle attached to it, and putting it to his lips, blew a shrill call. "There," said he, handing it to her, as he spoke, "it will make a sound baby can hear, at any rate, and the dog's head will amuse him." He put it into her hand, chain and all, and was gone before she could say anything.

Often afterwards the sound of the little silver whistle might be heard over the fields near the bailiff's house on a summer evening, accompanied by pretty peals of baby laughter, when the giver of it was far from any sight or sound that reminded him of home.

CHAPTER III.

LADY HALLINGFORD's house was in Palace Gardens, Kensington. She came up to town from her beloved castle, and its grand, shady, peaceful grounds every spring, not for her own sake, but for Grosvenor's. Grosvenor was the one remaining to her of three sons, and he was the worst of the three. The youngest had been a delicate, ailing lad, and only lived till he was thirteen, of weak disposition, and with few capabilities. The portrait of the eldest hung in Lady Hallingford's morning-room at the Castle, and was that of a tall, noble, thoughtful-looking youth of one-and-twenty. His death broke his father's heart, and Lady Hallingford was left with nobody

to live for but Grosvenor, who was then
eighteen, and going through a very fast
course at Oxford. He was as strong as a
horse, and had more health, more muscle,
and better promise of life than his father
and his two brothers had had among them.
Lord Hallingford was asthmatic, but Grosvenor's chest was like a drum; poor Lord
Annerley had had almost every fever that
flesh is heir to, and died of the last; but
Grosvenor had never been in a fever in his
life : little Edgar could not walk a mile
without being tired, but Grosvenor could
have run two (at that time), without losing
breath. He was stouter now, and older;
but no self-indulgence, no daring excess,
no recklessness, no carelessness had yet had
power to lay a weakening or withering
hand on the health and strength that had
been his best gift—a gift so utterly denied
to many purer and better men.

Lady Hallingford's disposition was so
bright, so hopeful — she was so loath to
dwell on the darkest and saddest points of
this world's picture, so ready to look out

and around for what was happiest and best in it—that, terrible as had been the blow of her eldest son's death, she would still have been a happy woman and mother if Grosvenor had been only a decently-conducted son and member of society. Not that she had anything to complain of in his manner towards herself : he was kind, and sometimes affectionate in private ; he was always respectful and considerate in public ; he let her be as much mistress as she liked at Hallingford, and he never asked any one to dinner of whom she did not approve.

But for all this, Grosvenor's life was a life into which she dared not look ; a life that made the burden and the sorrow of her naturally joyous heart ; a life that drew many scalding tears from eyes born to be bright, and to shed brightness on others ; a life which called forth many a beseeching prayer to Heaven, if haply at last the prodigal might return, saying, " Father, I have sinned !"

It did not seem to be the least Grosvenor's intention, however, ever to make this or any

other confession of repentance. He used to
say, in a general sort of way, that "he knew
he wasn't a good boy," but excused himself
on the ground of his father's having been a
roué before him. This mode of referring to
his father Lady Hallingford always found
terribly hard to bear. Why she had loved
her husband, and why he had loved her,
had always been a riddle to her friends;
and, to tell the truth, perhaps to herself
also. When a girl, she had been accustomed to spend a few weeks in every year
with her godmother, a woman of good
family, though of only small property, a
widow, and a widow who liked society.
At one or two dinners, and at a county-
ball, at a meet, at church, and once in a
long lane, where he met her on horseback
(she walking, and with her parasol full of
hedge-flowers), Miss Longley saw and " con-
quered" her future husband, then Lord
Annerley.

Why a dissipated man of nearly forty
fell in love with, and married, a natural,
happy, warm-hearted, intelligent girl of

two and twenty, it is, perhaps, not over-
whelmingly difficult to imagine ; but why
she, who had heart, sense, piety, and as-
pirations after everything that was noble
and good, fell in love with and married
him, God knows !

Of course, every one said it was for his
title. Well—perhaps it was. She would
have rejected the accusation herself with
indignant scorn ; but is there any woman
who can lay her hand upon her heart and
swear that, in no remotest corner of it,
there has ever laid the feeling that she
could marry a man who would place a
coronet on her head, if he were rich—if he
were tolerably good-looking, *and if he loved
her*, even though he fell short of her every
"lofty imagining" in other points ? There
may be such women ; there are of course
thousands of married women who would
declare that nothing on earth should have
induced them to do it, but how many young
women are there ? Theodora Longley was
a young woman, and a very good, and true,
and modest one ; and under no undue in-

fluence from her parents, and only a little from her godmother, yet she accepted and married the heir to the earldom of Hallingford, knowing—or at least guessing—that he was far from perfect, and was now paying that bitter price for so doing, which so many good women pay in sorrow and in secret (as far as they *can* do it in secret), every year of their after lives.

If Lady Hallingford had not surrounded herself with earnest interests of all kinds, she would have found this yearly recurring London season insufferably trying and disappointing. We say " disappointing," because her dearest wish in life was to see Grosvenor married and settled ; and Grosvenor was obstinate in refusing either to marry or to settle.

" Why, won't Lady Mary do for you ?" his mother asked one day, after they had been discussing this rather sore subject, during the whole time that my lord carved a small bull-dog out of a bit of box wood.

A rough species of wood-carving, be it said, which owed its origin to a youthful habit of disfiguring the trees in his father's park, was Grosvenor's one artistic taste on earth.

" She's too stout and too old, mother."

" Why, she's only seven-and-twenty, and you are over thirty. How many more years, Grosvenor, do you intend me to go on cudgelling my brains to find out suitable matches for you, which you reject one after another, in exactly the order I propose them ?"

"Never mind, mother ; look at my dog," said his lordship. " Isn't he a beauty, and doesn't he stand well ?"

" Do be serious for once, Grosvenor."

" Well, I am. Go on. Who's next on the list ?"

" Do you like Lord Belton's second daughter ?"

" Clara, with the red hair ?"

"Yes."

" Pretty well. Sometimes I think I shall make up to her."

" I wish you would. She is a very good girl.".

(Query — How is it that these good mothers of bad sons never think any woman's happiness too precious to be risked on the chance of reforming the one darling but sinning object of their own solicitude and tears ? They blame other women who sacrifice their daughters to roués ; but they look eagerly and anxiously around, to find a wife for their own especial roué, and think they are fulfilling one of the highest and most sacred duties of a mother !)

" I think she's rather a jolly girl, myself," was Lord Hallingford's candid admission, " but I don't know that I've much chance. I asked her to dance the other night, but she was engaged to her cousin, and I asked her to dance last night, but she was engaged to some one else."

" Well, perhaps she was — really,— Grosvenor."

" Oh, I don't doubt for a moment that she was. Only, she looked precious glad that she could say so, that's all I mean." And Lord Hallingford began whistling as he put one or two additional touches to his dog's back.

" What the deuce do I want with being married at all ?" pursued he, after a few minutes' silence, during which his mother continued her occupation of tearing up old letters.

" Well, Grosvenor, I suppose you don't wish to be the last Earl of Hallingford, do you ?" inquired my lady, with some warmth.

" Why, it doesn't follow that I shouldn't be, because I got married. Look at that fellow Longley. He's got a pretty little wife enough ; but the estate's going out of the family for all that, unless she dies and he gets married again. Best thing she could do, too."

" Don't you think they are happy then ?" asked Lady Hallingford, looking at her son rather closely as she spoke, and suspending the tearing-up process.

" Oh, I don't know. There's a little game going on in that quarter, which I'm rather interested in watching; that's all."

" What sort of game ?"

" Oh ! . . . . she's in love with that

handsome fellow, Ernest Glanville : it's a clear case. I flirted with her a little myself last season ; but I only did it from good-nature, you know, to give her prestige, and by George, it did give it her! I say, mother, you should go and see her picture in the Royal Academy, it's killing! All the fellows are talking about it."

" I have been—went last week. But what were you saying about———"

" Oh, I was only going to say I should have been afraid of having my head pounded to a jelly, if I'd ever gone half the lengths Mr. Glanville does. My attachment was Platonic entirely, and beautifully innocent."

" Are you joking, Grosvenor ?" inquired Lady Hallingford, speaking in a voice he hardly knew.

" No, I'm not joking. I never was more serious in my life."

" What does he say ? What does he do ?"

" He doesn't say or do anything," returned her son ; " at least, nothing particular. That's the beauty of it. Never saw any-thing better conducted in my life. Only an old hand like myself could find out there was anything wrong."

" Anything wrong ?" repeated Lady Hallingford, in a voice of such consternation and terror that Grosvenor looked up at her, and eyed her for several seconds.

" Oh, it was only my nonsense," he said, getting up, and pushing the litter of his wood-carving to the other side of the table. " Glanville is an acknowledged flirt, that's all ; and she likes him, or his singing—it's all the same thing."

" Is that all you meant ?"

"Of course it is. Only I went on because I saw you took it so seriously. And even if she does like him, it won't do Longley a bit of harm to have his confounded pride taken down, by seeing there are other fellows in the world besides himself. He nods to me when he drives past as if he were a Duke and I hardly worth noticing. However, I've wasted time enough here now, mother, so I'm off."

" If that fellow weren't so deucedly rude to me," said Lord Hallingford to himself, as he descended the stairs, " I might have done him a good turn by telling my mother the truth ; but as it is, he may see to his own concerns. Besides, it's hardly regrettable : he will get a divorce, marry again, and not have his grey hairs brought with sorrow, &c., by reflecting that Riverswood will come to me. Hollo, Longley !— ' talk of the '—I beg your pardon, but I was just thinking of you. How are you ?" and Lord Hallingford held out his hand with a peculiar and rather mocking smile on his face.

" I have only three minutes to see Lady Hallingford," said his cousin, hurriedly. " Can I see her, now ?"

Grosvenor tossed his head slightly in the direction of the staircase, and said,

" All right. Her ladyship's reading-room, Trevilyan. There's no one there."

Lady Hallingford rose hastily as her nephew was shown into the room, and then sat down again. Her manner and expression were so strained, her greeting so devoid of its natural frankness and geniality, that Rochefort must have noticed and wondered at the change if he had not been too preoccupied to notice anything.

" I have come to ask a kindness of you, Aunt Theodora. Shall you be much occupied the next few days ?"

" Not more than usual, Rochefort. You know my time is always full."

" I know it is ; but I am going down to Riverswood, and leaving my wife alone, and I want you to be so good as to look in upon her now and then : and should you mind taking her with you to two or three places she is going to—that is, of course, if you are going yourself ? She does not quite like giving them up."

" She ought to give them up, Rochefort. She does not look fagged as she did last season, but she looks over-excited and over-strained, and that is worse. A rest would do her good."

" She will not rest," answered her husband, rising and holding out his hand ; " but Lady Hallingford, I have not told you yet why I am leaving her."

"I supposed it was on some matter of business."

"No; I wish it was. I have just had a telegram that my mother is dangerously ill."

"Dangerously! What do you think it is?"

"I am told, you see," he answered, unfolding the paper, and holding it before her; "acute congestion of the liver. I must not stay, however; the train starts at three, and I am going home again first, for five minutes."

"Can Nora come and lunch with me tomorrow?" said her ladyship.

"I will ask her. Many thanks. God bless you, Aunt Theodora, for all you have been to us—to me especially!"

They kissed each other, Lady Hallingford being in tears, and then wished goodbye.

"I hope to God that was only random talk of Grosvenor's," said his aunt to herself after he had left her.

Nora was lying on one of her drawing-

room sofas when her husband came back
and bounded up the staircase for a last em-
brace and a few last words. They had never
been parted yet since their wedding-day.

It was very hot, and she had the windows open, to let in the air and the scent
of flowers from the balconies. She was
fanning herself, and smelling patchouli from
a little gold and diamond' scent-bottle.
Dressed in white muslin, with two roses
nestling among the lace, with a background
to her figure of lace and satin window
hangings and green - house plants, and
fluttering her spangled white fan, Mrs.
Rochefort looked very lovely, and knew
that she did.

"I have only a moment more, my darling," said her husband, throwing himself
on his knees beside her. "Kiss me—kiss
me again."

"Come back as soon as you can, and
give poor mamma my love," said his wife.

"There is nothing you want me to bring
you, is there?"

"No, dear, nothing, thank you. There—

don't be late for your train It would be
dreadful if you were."

"I know—I must go now. Kiss me
once more. You will promise me to take
care of yourself?"

"I will be very good ; I will, indeed.
There, my dear boy, do be off! You would
never forgive yourself if you missed that
train."

He was down in the hall, and on the
point of jumping into his cab, when he
heard his wife call out suddenly from the
landing above,

"Rochefort—Rochefort! Are you gone?"

"No, I am here. What is it?"

"Bring me my turquoises from the little
drawer behind the right-hand glass door of
my wardrobe—the locket, and brooch, and
ear-rings; I have the bracelet. Don't forget."

"I won't forget, my darling. You are
sure there is nothing else?"

"Nothing, thanks. Good-bye."

She went back into the drawing-room,
and her husband kissed his hand to her for
the last time, as she stood at the window,
and watched him to the turn of the street.

CHAPTER IV.

THAT evening there was a reception at Lady Belton's. The next night, the Countess of Hallingford had a dance.

" Don't go to Erminia's to-night," said Lady Hallingford, when she called on Nora about five o'clock, and was taking a cup of tea on the sofa at her side. " I will make your excuses. You will be fresher for dancing to-morrow if you rest to-night. You are not inured to our town life yet, you country blossom," she added, in her kind, pleasant way, "and we must take care of you."

There were two or three gentlemen present—one of them Mr. Glanville, who had only just entered, and went five minutes after. It was not his habit to come on Nora's receiving afternoons, but he had been passing, and found the temptation irresistible. He had been near when Lady Hallingford spoke, and although engaged and apparently absorbed in conversation with an eminent medical man, and Nora's doctor, heard each word, and now turned slightly round, saying,

"I think you are right, Lady Hallingford—Mrs. Longley is not made of hard enough stuff for this killing life."

"Oh, nonsense," said the medical man, "Mrs. Longley is getting as strong as any of us. She is taking my advice; and, of course, the direct consequence is, that her health is becoming perfect."

Ernest laughed, and turning away, began talking to one of the ladies. Lady Hallingford soon rose to go.

"Then you won't be good?" she said, as she shook hands.

"Dear Lady Hallingford, you are so very kind, and I am so much obliged to you. But it would be dreadfully lonely for me, you see, to stay at home when Rochefort is only just gone. I shall not stay more than a couple of hours;" after which Lady Hallingford went.

About half an hour before dinner-time, Mr. Glanville's cab drove up a second time to No. 13, Eden Street, and he said to the man who opened the door,

" I dropped a new lemon-coloured kid glove here. You hav'n't happened to see it, have you?"

" No, sir; I have not. Did you drop it in the hall, sir?"

" I thought I did, or on the stairs; but if you hav'n't seen it, I must have left it in the drawing-room. I shall be back in a moment," he called out to his man, " but keep the horse moving. You've driven her too fast," and he sprang up the stairs.

" Have you seen the glove, Henry?" asked one footman of the other, as he leant negligently against the wall, awaiting Mr. Glanville's return.

" No, nor has anybody else, it's my belief."

" How long should you say it'll tak
looking for ?"

" Well, my lady's going out at half-past
nine," returned the other, " and it's just
gone half-past six.   Say twenty minutes to
dress—that leaves us an hour and three-
quarters all but five minutes for the glove.
Stop, I'd forgotten about the dinner."

" I thought you gave them time enough,"
said the other.   And then both the men
laughed.

" When'll master be back ?" asked one,
presently.

" More than you or I can guess, my boy.
Perhaps in a week—or perhaps ten days."

" He'd better not be much longer, I
fancy," returned the other. " By George !—
here he is down again ! Well, I'm blowed !"

" It took an hour and a half to find the
letter the week before last," muttered
Henry, as he moved away.

As Mr. Glanville walked through the
hall, he put something into the man's hand.

" To buy yourself a few cigars with," he
said, carelessly.

"Thank you, sir; much obliged to you, sir."

"Look here, Henry," said the man, two minutes afterwards, when the cab was gone, and the door shut—showing what lay in his hand.

"Good gracious; that looks bad, it strikes me," returned Henry, regarding it with a very peculiar expression.

"Looks like another, I fancy, before the season's over," laughed the first.

"No, I shall have the next. It's me as opens the drawing-room door; you'll remember that, my buck."

"Ah, but only when missis receives; and Mr. Glanville always calls Mondays and Saturdays, so you're out there."

"He'll have to stump up for me, too, though, you'll see," retorted the other, and then the two parted.

Why did Ernest sing "Di Provença" that night? or why was not some pitying spirit at hand to divest his marvellous voice of some of its relentless and thrilling power over the woman who loved him with all the infatu-

ated love of which her nature was capable?
Lady Hallingford, like the brave lady that
she was, risked making herself hateful for
ever, by forging an excuse to get Nora into
the picture-room just when she saw Mr.
Glanville was going to sing. "There was
a water-colour she especially wished to show
her, which Clara Belton had said was just
like a corner of the park at Riverswood.
Would she come and tell her what she .
thought of it?" Nora came, holding up
from the 'destroying' tread of man her dress
of pale green silk and white lace; and with
pearls and emeralds on her neck and arms,
and pearls and a soft white feather in her
masses of fair hair (it was not all her own,
as we have said before), she looked very
beautiful. Men made a kind of "worship"
of her wherever she appeared; and it was,
perhaps, the easy combination of grace,
dignity, and yet gaiety, with which she
received their homage that had made
Ernest feel, with fatal power, the charm of
her entire difference of manner towards
himself. It was, however, as Lord Hal-

lingford said, " only to an old hand in such matters " that this difference of manner was perceptible. She talked almost less to Mr. Glanville than to anyone else in society; when she did talk to him it would be in a low voice, now and then with a sort of trembling reserve about her; at other times uttering sudden little confidences, which he believed she would have uttered to no one ·else, and which he heard with a wildly beating heart; confidences which, worthless as they were, he treasured up, and took away with him, as one would treasure and hold fast jewels gathered from under the feet of a careless, noisy, hurrying throng.

Ernest was too much of a gentleman in manner, and (in a certain sense) in feeling too, to compromise any woman he cared about, by too great a display of attention in society. And thus it came to pass that the state of feeling between himself and Nora had grown to be an infatuation on her part, and a passion on his, without either the world at large or her husband being aware that there was anything more between

them than the usual and almost unavoid-
able liking of a young fellow for a very
lovely woman—and his friend's wife; and
of a young woman for an exceedingly handsome, agreeable, and accomplished young
man—and her husband's friend.

Although Lady Hallingford kept her
niece engaged in looking at that picture till
Mr. Glanville's song was well over, she could
not prevent every note of the rich voice
reaching them, where they stood; its rise
and fall, only softened—and perhaps to one
of them rendered only more thrilling—by
the distance.   When they re-entered the
music-room—where the crowd was momen-
tarily increasing, as was the case everywhere
else—Ernest took the opportunity of Lady
Hallingford's being engaged in conversation
with a certain bishop, whose every word he
knew she would treasure as gold and silver,
too precious to be lost, and moved slowly
up to Nora's side.   Making a place for himself against the wall a little behind her, and
fixing his eyes, not on her, but on a marble
group just opposite, he said—

"You were not in the room just now, when I sang."

"Did you know that?"

"Of course I did." . . . .

After two minutes silence—

"Are you staying here long?"

"No, I promised to go early, on account of Aunt Theodora's dance to-morrow night."

Just at this time Lady Belton passed them, leaning on a gentleman's arm. When she saw Nora she "drew up" for a moment.

"I wanted to see you again, Mrs. Rochefort. You will be sure and let me know what news you have had from Riverswood, as soon as you have any?—Thanks, I shall be very anxious to know.—Ah, Mr. Glanville! thank you so much for that lovely song of yours. You will sing once more for me to-night? Please don't say no."

"I should be delighted, Lady Belton, but I have two other engagements, and I must be going in ten minutes." And then her ladyship moved on.

"Where are you going, Mr. Glanville?" asked Nora. "Home," he answered.

" Home?"

" Yes. Have you not just told me that you were not going anywhere else to-night ?" And then at last he turned his eyes on her.

A minute or two afterwards, Lady Hallingford was seen to move, and Mr. Glanville was in another part of the room when she came up.

As the Countess put down her niece in Eden Street, about twelve o'clock, she said,

" Of course, my dear, if you should have any worse news to-morrow, though I sincerely hope there is no chance of it,—I shall not expect you. But you will let me know, will not you ?"

" Certainly, Lady Hallingford. Thank you very much. . . . Good night."

" Good night ;" and Lady Hallingford drove away.

The following afternoon there came a telegram from Rochefort. He said, " My mother is still ill, but the doctor assures me there is no danger yet. She is very nervous, and will not hear of my leaving her. Have already written to you. Hope you keep well."

Nora went to the dance, exquisitely dressed, and dazzling with her diamonds and rubies. She danced a great deal, and went home rather late.

" How well, and how *very* lovely Rochefort's wife looks to-night !" said Clara Belton to her sister, a half-sigh escaping from her lips and her true heart as she spoke.

"She has danced too often with Mr. Ernest Glanville," replied the practical Erminia ; " mamma has been noticing it, and so have other people, I believe. I have just been dancing with Lord Hallingford ; Nora and Mr. Glanville were in the next set, and he looked in a way I didn't like at them."

" I can't bear Lord Hallingford," rejoined Clara, colouring, and with some fierceness.

" I don't like him ; but I don't think a married woman should flirt," responded Mrs. Templeton, as she walked away.

About two o'clock, Mrs. Longley, leaning on the arm of her last partner ; took her leave of her hostess.

" Your carriage is here, my child ?"

" Oh yes, Lady Hallingford, thank you ; and you see I am not at all done up."

" No, indeed ; and you have been dancing
a great deal more than you ought—I am
afraid.   Mr. Cavendish, you are sure I can
trust you to see my niece safely to her
carriage ?   I have made myself responsible
to her husband for her well-being."

" I will forfeit your friendship for life,
Lady Hallingford, if I do not see Mrs. Long-
ley well cloaked and well coached," replied
Mr. Cavendish, laughing.

("Why are some men always trying to
be funny, and to make puns ?" muttered
her ladyship, as she turned away.)

When Nora's brougham had moved about
thirty yards from the house, a gentleman
suddenly stopped it ; saying, " Is that Mrs.
Longley's carriage ?" and the coachman
drew up.   The speaker opened the door ;
spoke a few hurried words in an under-
tone ; and then with his foot on the step,
looked up at the coachman and said, " Mrs.
Longley will take me as far as Eden Street.
I can't find my cab.   James must have got
drunk I suppose, somewhere."

CHAPTER V.

MRS. LONGLEY'S illness was severe, and for
some days dangerous; and her son stayed
with her nearly three weeks. During this
whole time, she was nervous, exacting, and
low-spirited to excess; and at any hour if
she felt herself the least worse, would send
emissaries all over the estate to recall him
to her bed-side. At last, when she was
pronounced decidedly convalescent (though
still ailing, and requiring great care), her son
represented to her that he could not leave
his wife alone any longer. They would soon
be back now, he said;—and as he spoke the
words, his heart rejoiced at the idea of ex-
changing Eden Street, and nights spent at
balls and receptions, for his cherished park

and fields, and the fresh, pure hay-and-blossom-scented air of the country.

A day or two after his determination had been taken, Rochefort returned to town by a late train, and then drove home at once. " Don Giovanni," was being played that night, with a splendid " cast ;" and he had telegraphed to his wife not to miss it, but to go with Lady Hallingford. Lady Hallingford never heard but three operas, and " Don Giovanni," was one of them. Nora however, did not go with her to this especial representation.

After he had had his supper, the master went up with his paper to his wife's dressing-room, where there was a small fire. It had been wet and chilly the last day or two ; and Mrs. Rochefort, who was somewhat inclined to be "shivery" when she came home at night, liked the cheerful light and warmth of a fire to undress by, if the thermometer showed the least diminution of temperature.

Her husband seated himself in her little velvet arm-chair, with his *Times,* and

read for some time. Suddenly, he remembered that he had put her " turquoises "
into an inner pocket of his coat, with some
letters and papers, at the last moment before leaving home; and he felt rather hastily
in his pocket, to make sure that they were
safe. Then he thought he would lock them
up at once for her, and have done with them;
and throwing down his paper, got up and
walked across the room to her dressing-
table. He had duplicate keys to all his
wife's wardrobes and jewel cases, in case of
hers ever being mislaid or lost; and now
he took a small bunch of keys out of his
waistcoat pocket, and selecting one, turned
the lock of a handsome ivory casket, which
stood on the table. He found the little
velvet-covered tray at the top, already filled
with jewels; and so lifted it, and placed
the locket, brooch, and ear-rings, in one of
the little cells beneath. There was a small
pocket, or case, at the side of the box;
forming part of the lining, and meant to
hold bank notes, or any other small papers
of value or importance. Rochefort would

not have noticed it, but that it seemed full; the papers within preventing the pocket from closing. Partly because he had nothing else to do, and partly because he had a very pardonable curiosity to see whether any of his own letters were among the documents thus carefully preserved, he drew the papers out, and began examining them. There were two or three bills, a little scented " sachet " or two, a lock of hair, lighter than his own, tied with silk, and inclosed in half a sheet of his wife's thick, glossy, scented note paper ; and some letters.

The letters had come through the post, the last bearing the date of only the day before, and they were directed in Ernest Glanville's hand-writing.

When a man is shot by musket-fire, through the heart, only a momentary contortion passes over him ; he feels but the agony of an instant—there is, perhaps, one terrible start, and then rigid stillness and coldness for evermore !

But when the shot comes from the mere

sight of anything before the eyes, or the mere sound of anything taken in by the ears, the lengthened agony endured by the heart into which such a ball has sped, is unutterable by any words in any human tongue.

Rochefort could not at first move, or breathe, under the suddenness of his shock; a physical spasm seemed to contract his heart ; his hands—rigid, as if icy cold had paralysed them—held, without feeling that they held, those fatal letters. By a desperate effort of will—the blood, which at first seemed frozen in his veins, becoming free, and rushing hot, headlong, and furious, through his trembling frame—he read those letters word by word, and each one of them to the end.

When he had finished, he crushed them in his hand, flung them upon the floor, and ground them with his furious heel. He cursed their writer :—as he walked like a madman up and down the room, he cursed himself; he raved against his bitter fate, his lost love, his blasted life, knowing hardly what he did or said, or if there was any God, or any heaven, or any goodness left, in his awful woe and shame.

He was walking still—and the letters were lying soiled and trampled, where he had first cast them down,—when the door opened, and his wife—in her radiant dress—in the full light of her radiant beauty, diamonds upon her breast and on her arms—the full, white, lovely breast and arms he had folded to his own, and covered with his pure, passionate kisses so often—stood before him, and stood thunderstruck. In that moment she saw what he knew, and how he knew it; and as he turned his face on her, vivid with expressions of dread, horror, anger, desolation, she threw up her arms, and with one piercing cry, fell face foremost and in a heap upon the threshold.

Every servant in the house rushed upstairs at that terrible sound. They were all standing pale, amazed, terrified, and questioning each other, when the master's voice silenced them all.

" Carry your mistress into her room," he said.

She had not fainted : that poor mercy had not been granted her ; she lay, groaning and writhing and suffering in every nerve of both heart and body. They lifted her, and laid her on her bed, and she kept her face hidden from their sight with her folded arms.

" Cover me over," she said to her maid. " Cover me—over my head, and face, and feet—everywhere ! And put the lights out, and leave me in the dark, for God's sake !"

    *   *   *   *

" Where is Saunders ?" said the master when her door was shut ; " I want to see him."

" Gone home, sir," said one of the men. Saunders was the coachman.

" Gone home ? Gone to the devil ! Go, one of you, instantly, and send him here."

" He's only at the stables," whispered one footman to the other. " Shall I tell him ?"

" What do you mean by talking to each other ?" shouted Rochefort, " go and do my bidding, and send Saunders to me."

One of them was obliged to go, and after about ten minutes, Saunders appeared, looking as if he had come to hear his death-warrant. When he came, Rochefort locked himself into the dining-room with the man, and sent everyone else in the house to their beds. No one knew what happened, or what was said on either side.

About half past one, when the miserable coachman reached his home, as pale as death, and with the tears coursing each other down his cheeks, he seated himself on a rickety chair at the foot of his wife's bed, one tallow candle lighting the little room, and told his wretched tale.

" I never did see a man in such a taking in all my life, Polly. It's just as if he'd gone mad. I wish I'd never seen the colour of that cursed fellow's money, that I do ! And I always liked the master, you know I did, and now I feel as if I'd been and murdered him."

" I don't know whatever we shall do," groaned his wife. ´ " You've been and lost

your character, and we're ruined. Oh dear
me !—dear me !"

" He says," pursued poor Saunders, his
face retaining the same awe-struck pallor
and rigidity it had worn since the moment
of his being summoned to his master's presence—" Mr. Glanville says to me, ' Saunders,' he says, ' you mustn't think there's
anything wrong about this, don't imagine
such a thing ; but we're old friends, and we
never get a chance of a word in company.
Only don't say anything about it for your
life, for her husband might cut up rough
about it, you know.' You fancy a gentleman like him talking to me like that ? But
bless you, these fine fellows, they'll do anything, I've seen that. They're no better
than us—often a deal worse." After a
little time, the man continued, " You see,
Polly, it was ten shillings in my pocket
every time he came home in that carriage ;
and his man—he thought he walked from
places. ' Well, Saunders,' says he to me one
day, ' what do you think of this new dodge
of my governor's, walking home from

parties ?   I'm getting quite a holiday, I can tell you,' he says.

"'Oh, he walks home from parties, does he ?' says I.

"'Yes ; don't you know ?   Says he ain't well, and that he must have more exercise. I haven't fetched him 'ome from anywhere these ten days.'

" I never said a word, no more than a statoo.   I've never said a word to a livin' bein' ; and I've got all those 'arf sovereigns still : only five shillings as I spent one day over that cap for the baby."

" You've got them all still ?" repeated his wife, anxiously.

"Yes ; and I'm going to send every farthing of 'em back," replied the man, striking his hand upon his knee ; " I shall never forget to my dying day, what I've seen and heard this night.   I hope I shall be forgiven, that's all."

" I don't see as you were so much to blame," said the poor woman, who had cried her eyes almost out of her head, " not after what the gentleman said to you."

" Do you think I believed that gammon ?"
inquired poor Saunders, with a touch of
contempt in his voice. " I knew better
than that. There was one day," he continued, " I drove her to Victoria Station,
and I was to call for her at five minutes to
eight, punctual, in the evening. I'd a pretty
good idea of what was up. And there was
two other days she went to Clapham, to
see 'a friend who had just lost a parient,' or
something ; and she wouldn't drive there,
as it was so 'ot for the 'orses, but she'd go
by train. Her maid told Hewitson that,
and Hewitson told me, and Hewitson and I
laughed about it ; but I didn't appear to
know nothink. She got into the carriage,
dressed in black, and with a veil on, and a
sort of a mauvy bonnet, as I'd never seen
her in before, and I took her to the station,
and was to come for her same time as
before."

" Well, you were no way to blame taking
her to the station : no one can say that,"
asserted his wife.

" No, of course, it wasn't I as could refuse

to drive her about to every station in
London, if she'd wanted to go ; but what
does it signify talking ?" ended the wretched
coachman, as he rose at last from his chair ;
" it's done now ; but as long as ever I live,
I'll never be concerned in such an affair
again, no, not for a hundred pounds !"

     ✻   ✻   ✻   ✻

Rochefort paced the floor of his dining-
room for the rest of that miserable night.
But towards six o'clock, exhausted by
fatigue, by agitation, and by grief, he threw
himself on the sofa, and slept heavily—slept
till long after the household was astir, and
the lovely light of a fresh, warm July
morning had shone behind the closed shutters and curtains of the room. When he
woke, with a groan, and with a feeling as if
he had lived a long, awful life since he slept
and woke last—a life in which some nameless ruin had befallen himself and the whole
world—he found it was close upon ten
o'clock. He unlocked and opened the door,
and went up to his dressing-room. In
crossing the landing he met his wife's maid.

She looked pale and haggard, and her eyes were swelled with crying.

" Is your mistress in her room ?" inquired the master, stopping for a moment.

" Yes, sir."

" See that she has all she wants, but do not leave her, and get everything packed up as soon as you can. We shall not be in the house after to-morrow."

" Going home, sir ?" asked the girl, in a faltering voice.

" No. Not home." It was all he said, and then passing her, he opened the door of his room. As he did so, a sudden thought seemed to strike him back ; and he turned away with the words, " Tell Henry to bring all my things for dressing into the red room."

He was occupied the whole of that day in making the necessary arrangements for leaving town, in writing, and in seeing his lawyer. With this latter gentleman, he arranged for his wife's being taken at once to Paris, and thence to any place of residence abroad she might choose. He gave him a large cheque on his banker, to meet every possible expense attending her journey, and made Mr. Stanley promise not to leave her, until he had seen her established in some suitable residence.

"Have you any suggestion to make as to place?" inquired the lawyer.

"No; you must be guided by her own wishes. The quieter and the more retired the position the better, of course. I do not feel capable of thinking of, or deciding on, anything at present," added the poor fellow, in an unsteady voice. "But I think you have travelled, Mr. Stanley? Heaton told me so once, I believe."

" Yes, in France," answered the lawyer; " nowhere else."

"That will do, of course. Well, then, Mr. Stanley, there are other things to settle. Let me see." He drew his hand across his forehead, as if confused. . . . . "I must either make her an annual allowance, of course, or settle some money on her, from which she can draw at will."

"Then," said Mr. Stanley, with a little

hesitation, "I presume there was no settlement made upon Mrs. Longley when she was married?"

"No," said Rochefort; "there ought to have been, but there was not. That was no one's fault but my own. I am afraid," he continued, with a faint smile, in which there was something pitiable, "I never thought of it. But the facts being as they are, I had better arrange with you about her having a certain annual allowance, and then . . . then you can explain everything to her when I am gone."

"It will certainly be better to make her an annual allowance, than to settle money upon her, under present circumstances," said the lawyer, with a slight emphasis in his tone. "And it ought to be an allowance dependent—excuse me for speaking plainly, Mr. Longley, it is my duty—dependent upon her conduct in future."

Rochefort coloured all over his pale face, and bit his under lip hard.

"I will leave the matter with you," he said, after a few minutes' silence. "You are in a better position to judge of things than I am."

He got up as he spoke, and took several turns in the room, struggling with emotion that, for the moment, was almost unconquerable.

" May I ask, Mr. Longley, what you intend to allow your wife ?" asked the lawyer at last. " I think you have not told me."

" Would —— hundred a year do ?   I should like her to have every comfort she can have, and not to be hampered in any way, in her choice of residence, and so on."

" It is a very generous sum.   Few men in your position would do as much," said the lawyer.   " Have you thought it all over well enough ?   Forgive my asking you."

" If you mean as to the money," returned Rochefort, " it is simply valueless to me. I mean, valueless as far as I myself am concerned.   I have, unhappily, no child ; and now I have no wife."

His voice broke over the last words ; and Mr. Stanley observed a sympathetic silence for several minutes.

After about half an hour, spent in the discussion of necessary business details of various kinds, the lawyer, putting down his pen, and looking up, said—

" May I ask what you are going to do, yourself, Mr. Longley ?"

" I am going out of the country to-morrow evening," returned Rochefort. " I wish I were gone now, but it is impossible. I have still many things to think of ;" and as Mr. Stanley rose, he gave him his hand in the weary, absent manner he had observed through all the last part of the interview.

" Mr. Longley, I am truly and deeply sorry for you," said the lawyer.

" I am sure you are, my dear fellow," returned Rochefort, moving by a sudden effort from the mantel-piece, against which he had been leaning. " I am sure you are. Good-night. Come here to-morrow, after I am gone, you know—and tell her about it; and—and—take her away. Don't miss the early train, Stanley, and then have the carriages about in broad day, for God's sake !" And after this they parted.

When all that he could do was done; when the streets were comparatively quiet, in the darkness of the tranquil summer night; when the ceaseless, unsympathetic roll of the carriages was over for a time, and there was no sound in the house, save a servant's occasional footstep, to break the oppressive stillness, Rochefort went out and wandered, he knew and cared not whither.

The thought that had come to be most terrible to him, was, that in the whole earth there was no redress to him for his wrong. The poor, half-starving man who stole a loaf or a coin could be punished, and was punished, with rigour; but this man, this " familiar friend," who had robbed him of all he held most sacred upon earth—who had laid, with ruthless hand, his whole future life in ruin before his face ; who had blasted his honourable name; who had flung a foul and irremediable stain upon an escutcheon upheld in bravery, in chivalry, and in honour for three hundred years—must go free, could not be touched by the arm of man, or brought to justice by the power of human law.

Not many years ago, there was one, and only one, revenge possible ; and Rochefort, in his present wild misery and bitter anger, would have given half his life-time, would have risked his life, for that one revenge to have been possible to him. He had a strong element in his blood of the old cavalier spirit of his family. And now, as he walked along, he clenched his impotent right hand, and cursed the cruel fate which left him powerless against the man who had so vilely wronged and so treacherously injured him. Rochefort had moods as different as dark night is different from sunny day, or as a raging fire is different from the glittering of a star. It was dark night with him now, and the raging fire was hot and dangerous within his breast. All day long he had bound down the demon of his anger and his hatred with strong chains—had resolutely drugged and smothered it. It was awake now, and had risen, and was rending him with fearful might.

*   *   *   *

It was after midnight when he reached

his house. There was unusual confusion within; the servants were all congregated in the hall, and on the stairs sat Agnes, his wife's maid, sobbing hysterically.

"What is all this?" asked the master, sternly; "what are you all doing?"

There was no immediate answer.

"What is it, I ask you?" repeated Roche-fort, furiously; "I will turn you every one out of the house, if you do not answer me."

"My mistress is gone, sir," replied the terrified maid.

"*Gone?*" repeated Mr. Longley. In spite of all the awful suffering he had been through, he felt now as if he were struck for the first time. "*Gone?*" he said again.

The housekeeper, who was trembling and deathly white, came up to him, and slightly touching his arm, said—

"Get her to come with you upstairs, sir. Don't let her speak here before the men."

They went upstairs. The door of Nora's room was open, and the master walked in and seated himself on an ottoman at the foot of her bed. He felt as if it was years since he had entered that room last, or since he had slept there, or seen her in it. Everything was in confusion. The lids of the half-packed trunks and boxes stood open; the sofa and chairs were strewed with silk and muslin and lace dresses; and the innumerable and almost useless articles of elegance and luxury, which it had been her extravagant fancy to collect for the adornment of her rooms, lay in heaps upon the tables or on the floor. A few hours ago her husband would have shrunk from the sight of a glove belonging to her; now, he looked on all these things as if sensation were dead within him; they did not move, they did not pain him; feeling had been wrung till it lay insensible; he seemed turned to stone.

"What there is to tell, tell me quickly," he said in a dull sort of voice, as he leaned his head upon his two hands; "then it will be all over . . . . . ."

"My mistress wrote a letter, sir, this afternoon," began the maid, in a broken and at first faltering voice, which however increased in steadiness as she went on, "and after she had written it she was very restless, and walked for a long time up and down the room. She kept on asking me, 'Agnes, where is it we are to go?' and I told her I knew nothing, but that we were going away to-morrow. At last she went to her desk again, and took an envelope and put her letter in, and directed and stamped it, and then told me to take it to the post for her. I said I dare not; and when she saw I was not to be persuaded, she locked it up, and began walking up and down the floor again. Then she helped me to pack away her jewels, and to fold some of her things; and then she would sit down on her chair and watch me, without speaking. At last she got up and said she was stifled in the room, and she must have the air somehow. The windows had been shut, all but the dressing-room window, but I opened them all, and then she seemed to be a little easier. At last she said, 'Agnes,' she said, 'I will give you anything I have, if you will take that letter for me;' and because she seemed so heart-broken, I began to think if I might venture. But then I thought how you had told me not to leave her, sir, and I did not know what mischief might come of the letter, so I told her I couldn't, not for anything she could give or pay me. She sat for a long time after that with her head on her hands, but at last she got up, and said, 'You are right, Agnes ; you must obey your master ;' and she took the letter from her desk, and tore it up, and lighted a candle, and burnt every bit of it. Then she would have me change her dress for her, and she put on a black silk ; and then she took her purse, and seemed to count the money she had in it, and she said, 'Don't pack my lace shawl, Agnes, I want it to travel in ; or this thick one,' and she chose one out, and laid it on her bed ; and she said she would wear her new mauve bonnet, but she made me put a black feather in it. Then she lay down quite quiet on the sofa, with her face to the wall, and said she would try and sleep a little. But she never did ; she kept sighing, and now and then moving the pillows, and I tried to go on with the packing. But it seemed as if in all the boxes there would not be half room for her things, and I got almost into despair. She only spoke to me once, and then she said, ' Agnes, where is your master, do you know ?' "

The poor girl, who had borne up with great difficulty in relating her story, now made a pause and broke out into sobs and tears ; but as no one spoke, the master sitting with his face buried in his hands, and motionless as before, she controlled herself after a few minutes to go on.

" Soon after you went out, sir, my mistress said to me, ' Agnes,' she said, ' would you get me something from the chemist's—something I want very much ?' I was frightened, and said ; ' From the chemist's, ma'am ?' ' Only what I have had before,' she said, ' to make me sleep. I will give you Dr. Earnshaw's prescription. You need not be afraid. If you don't get it for me I think I shall go mad. My head is just like a wheel—going round, and round, and

round!' I said I would go and ask one of
the men. 'No, for God's sake!' she said,
raising herself up, 'don't speak to one of
them for me. I don't want one of them to
do anything for me, or to have any message
from me.' Well, she begged so hard, that
at last I said, as the chemist's was near, I
would go for her; but I told her I was
risking a great deal, as you had ordered me
not to leave her. She said to me, in an
impatient sort of a way, 'What in heaven's
name did he think I was going to do with
myself? I shall be here when you come
back, you silly girl. Now, go quickly.' I
ran all the way to the chemist's, sir, and
back, and did not wait for them to make up
the medicine, and when I got back and
came in here, the room was empty, sir, and
she was gone. I ran downstairs and looked;
I asked the men, but they had not seen
her; only one of them, coming into the
hall a little before cook let me in downstairs, said he had felt rather a cool air,
and when he went up to the door he found
it an inch or two open; and so she must

have gone as soon as my back was turned, and never shut the door, that they might not·hear."

Totally overcome, the poor girl wept bitterly, and for some moments her hysterical sobbing was the only sound heard in the room.

"That is all, then," said the master, at last, with a calm which seemed awful to them—a calm no more resembling peace than the cold of death resembles sleep. He got up and looked in a strange, almost vacant way, round the room. "You are sure she had money with her?" he asked.

"Yes, sir, I am sure of that; and she must have thrown on the shawls she put ready for her journey, for they are both gone, and the bonnet I had ready for her too."

*　　　*　　　*　　　*

Rochefort walked out of the room, and downstairs and into the library, which was at the back of the house, and removed by a passage from the other rooms on that floor. It was dimly lighted, and at that hour of the night felt chill, and looked ghostly and desolate. He closed the door after him, and in a mechanical way walked up to the window, parted the curtains, and looked out on to the dark court for several minutes. Then turning, he faced the empty room, and in that same moment seemed to face the full, awful front of his sorrow, as if it came upon him with a blow from an unseen and powerful hand. In one overwhelming wave there surged over his heart the consciousness of his life's love wasted—of his future lorn and blank—of his present of unutterable woe and shame—and he flung himself upon the ground with a sudden tempest of sobs and tears.

" Nora—Nora ! Oh, my love—my wife ! . . . . Oh, my darling ! . . . my darling that I have loved !"

He had lain for an hour prostrate in his misery, shaken in every nerve by the violence of his weeping, when a sudden thought made him raise himself, choke back his tears, control his agony by an effort almost superhuman. He sprang wildly on to his feet.

" How do I know where she is gone ?
How do I know what she is going to do ?
My God !—and I have been fool enough to
lie here thinking only of myself !"

He rushed out of the room, and out of
the house. There were still cabs in the principal thoroughfares, and he persuaded a man
(by a strong bribe) who had just set down
his fare and was going home, to drive him
to Baronetcy Square, where the Glanvilles
lived. No one was up in the house, and
the man had to ring for several minutes
before anyone came.

At last, a footman came, and asked what
was the matter.

" Is Mr. Ernest Glanville here ? Has he
come home to-night ?" inquired Rochefort,
forcing himself to utter the name calmly,
which he had thought never to utter again
upon this earth.

" Mr. Ernest, sir ? No, sir, I believe not."

" Go, and find out for me, and come back
and tell me at once."

In a minute or two the man returned.

" No, sir ; Mr. Ernest has never been in

since he was driven out, about ten o'clock, sir."

" Where to ?"

" His boy says to Mrs. Cavendish's, sir, Grosvenor Square, sir."

" Go and ask his boy and the other men if they know whether any note, or message of any kind, has come for Mr. Ernest Glanville since he went out."

The footman returned with the answer, " No, sir ; there has been no message or note of any kind."

Rochefort took out his pocket-book, tore a sheet from it, and, by the glare of a lamp in the square, wrote these words :

" Dear Sidney,—Do you know anything about your brother, or why he is not in to-night ? I am waiting for your answer. For God's sake, send quickly."

" If Mr. Glanville is asleep, don't give him that," said Longley; "but find out whether he is or not."

" If I were to wake Mr. Glanville, sir, by waking his man," hesitated the footman, as he looked at, and turned the paper in his

hand, "my lady would put herself about
dreadfully, sir. We're ordered never, on
no account whatever, to disturb Mr. Glanville, or to go near his room after he's gone
upstairs."

"I will take the responsibility of this
awakening of him," replied Rochefort, impatiently ; "it is a matter of life or death,
and I cannot wait much longer. Go at
once."

After about five minutes, Sidney's answer came. He had been awakened by the
ringing and disturbance, and the footman
met his servant on the landing, coming to
inquire what it was about.

No ; Sidney knew nothing of his brother.
But he wrote. "He is often out very late,
it is nothing unusual. What on earth
is the matter? Cannot you send me
word ?"

Rochefort, to whom all this time of waiting and terrible suspense had been as fuel
added to an already raging fire, crushed
Sidney's answer into his pocket, sent away
the cab, and set off walking, he knew not

where, and almost as if his senses had left him.

All night long he walked the darkened and almost desolate London streets like a madman. He crossed and recrossed the bridges—pursued by a horrible idea, which he dare not form into words, even in his own mind; he looked over into the dark, broad, sullen waters—then shuddering, he turned away, and rushed down long roads; or turned this way and that; with no plan or purpose in his head, but that of finding her—as if it were possible !

He walked miles, in his mad, wild, fruitless search. Not till it was full day-light, did he turn towards home. The men had sat up all night, not knowing where he was, and when they saw him, they thought his reason was gone. One of them ran for a doctor. *   *   *   *

" Tell me where my wife is," was all he would say to him when he came; "tell me where my wife is, and I will do anything you wish."

Dr. Earnshaw, who already knew the

story—which was now beginning to spread like wild-fire through London, or rather that part of London with which it had anything to do ; took his brougham at a gallop to Baronetcy-square, and saw Sir Charles Glanville himself.   Poor Sir Charles was in a state of rage and indignation verging on apoplexy.   Lady Glanville was in tears and hysterics, on the breakfast-room sofa.   But they had seen and heard nothing of Ernest, since he left home about ten o'clock the night before. When Dr. Earnshaw returned with this message, he found Rochefort almost delirious.   They forced him to take a little brandy, they bound wet cloths round his head, and the doctor stayed with him for an hour longer.

" Sir Charles has promised to let you know, the instant he hears anything," said Dr. Earnshaw; "he has sent to all the hotels, and I have sent men to all the quays from which the steamers start. We cannot be long in hearing something.   Besides, this very delay in learning anything of Mr. Ernest Glanville's whereabouts, confirms me

in the belief that your wife is with him.
And now, my dear fellow, do be guided by
me and lie down ; and take this sedative,
or I won't answer for the consequences."

"I will take anything—I will do anything, I tell you, when I hear where my
wife is. Not before. You ought not to
keep me here now," he would say, starting
up, "every minute that I am here is lost
time !" His head was gone.

The doctor was obliged to leave him,
but returned about two o'clock. While he
was in the house, a messenger arrived in
haste from Sir Charles Glanville's with a
note, which ran as follows :—

"Your wife is safe. Ernest has written
to Sidney from the —— Hotel ; where
he was summoned by a note from Mrs.
Longley, about half-past ten, last night.
No note was ever brought here, it must
have been taken after him, where he was.
They are leaving England."

"I never before," said Dr. Earnshaw,
when he related the events of the morning
to his wife after dinner ; "I never before

saw a man faint, with the relief of hearing that his wife was leaving England with the man who had ruined her."

"Poor fellow!" exclaimed Mrs. Earnshaw; "what is he doing now? What a terrible thing it has been!"

"I tried to persuade him to stay quietly in the house over another night, and get some rest," said the doctor; "but it was useless talking. I managed to drug a glass of port wine for him a little—without his knowing it—and he had a couple of hours of something like unconsciousness — not sleep—on the sofa. He would not go upstairs. He told me, he felt as if the murdered body of his wife lay stretched out in her room, and he could not go near it."

Mrs. Earnshaw shuddered.

"What has he done then?" she asked.

"He is going off this evening by the same boat he intended to leave by. He says he will rest on the other side of the water, and perhaps he will. He has left directions with his lawyer and the housekeeper to pack up everything, send

off the servants, and the rest of it. . . .
It's been an awful affair," ended the doctor,
getting up from his chair; "I shouldn't
like to see a man in such a state every day."

"Nor hear of a woman doing such a
wicked, shameful thing every day, either,"
exclaimed his wife with indignation; "she
is thoroughly bad, that's what *I* think.
And I hope she'll come to a bad end of some
sort or other; no punishment could be too
great for a woman who has left such a
husband."

"Only let us wait till we get the ladies
into parliament," said the doctor, looking
down at his wife with a good deal of amusement in his face; "that will be the time for
severe laws."

"Ah! but we shall make severe laws for
the men, too," pronounced Mrs. Earnshaw;
"don't forget that, sir. Have you had your
second glass of sherry, Arthur? Because if
you have, we will go into the drawing-room.
. . . Dear, dear! I shall think of this
affair for a week! What a beauty she was!
and he seemed such a nice fellow!"

CHAPTER VI.

PEOPLE took the great scandal of Mrs. Rochefort Longley's elopement in different ways. Some laid all the blame on the lady, and said she was a beautiful, unprincipled flirt, and could never have had heart or brain enough to be Rochefort Longley's wife. He was, perhaps, well rid of her, if he could only be brought to think so. And already the mammas of two, three, or four daughters, who had for months, or for years past, been wasting their substance on riotous living, to achieve the end (not yet, alas! achieved) of getting these same daughters "off," began to speculate on Mr. Longley's presently suing for a divorce, and re-appearing in Belgravia next season, in the character of a rich young bachelor, on the look out for a wife. Every lawyer or barrister (within a certain circle), if he went to a party, was quite certain to be asked during the course of the evening, " what were his opinions on the subject of divorce ; and whether he did not think it almost certain that poor young Longley would," &c., &c., &c.

Some people, of course, laid all the blame on the gentleman ; especially those families in which there were daughters to whose charms Mr. Glanville had always proved himself obstinately and blindly insensible.

" I never liked that young man," mamma would affirm, though she knew she would at any time have laid herself down for him to walk over, if that would have paved the way to his dancing a few times with one of her girls, or otherwise paying them attention. (Ernest was, of course, the prospective heir to the baronetcy ; Sidney's invalidism and spinal complaint making it next to impossible that he should ever marry).

"He was always a dreadful flirt," one young lady would observe.

"And I never thought him so excessively handsome," said a second, thereby recklessly and shamelessly perjuring herself. "He was quite over-rated, I think!"

"His voice was certainly lovely; but then he never would join our musical society, so I don't think much of him," would be the assertion of a third; "and he's done just what I should have imagined him capable of doing, from his whole style and manner."

"Confounded good-looking fellow, but too fast," the men said to each other at their clubs; "and he was such a fool to write letters."

(It was observed by some people, when the next season came on, that certain young fellows, of from twenty to thirty, seemed to have resolved "with one accord," to try and personate Mr. Ernest Glanville, to the best of their ability, now that he was fairly out of the field, and, for the present, would be "seen no more." They tried to imitate his languid way of leaning against a door-way or wall, at a dance, when he ought to have been dancing ; the cool, easy turn of his dark eyes (they practised the turn before their glasses, but they could not get the eyes) on some man shorter than himself, or some woman for whom he did not care; his manner of brushing his hair, of wearing his moustache, of fastening a diamond stud in his collar, just above the knot of his half-inch-wide white tie, of lifting his hat, of holding his partner in a waltz. His singing they could not copy ; that "sweet" voice would be " heard no more in Israel " (alias in London society), and the loss of it was mourned by the women, sincerely, and in concert.

There were some deep-seeing people, who laid the blame of this " dreadful affair" on the husband.

" I always thought he was a haughty looking fellow," Mrs. A. B. observed one morning over the breakfast-table ; " I dare say his wife wasn't happy with him. Perhaps, he'd an awful temper, perhaps he scolded her for spending too much money !"

(Mr. A. B. was observed to look cowed at this juncture, and to swallow his toast with precipitation; and after breakfast, when he and his son went out together, he said, " Took your mother's remark, did you, Frank—eh? Well, I'm dashed if I'd blame any man for scolding his wife for spending money. I believe that's what women are made for. Don't you marry, Frank, as long as you can keep out of it.")

" Always had such a cool way of looking at a fellow if you met him, that's what I didn't like," says Frank, pulling his moustaches before the looking-glass. " Never smiled any more than the Duke of ——. He'd splendid horses, but then other people have splendid horses besides him."

" He'd a beautiful smile when he did smile," said the eldest sister—Miss Araminta A. B.

" And do you know, I've seen him pick up a parcel for a poor old crippled man in Piccadilly," said a younger one, " and it was just in front of the Marchioness of Dash's carriage, with her footmen and coachman looking on. He was a very shabby looking old man, too, and could hardly drag himself along ; and I believe there was bacon in that parcel, it looked like it ; and Mr. Longley had pale, new kid gloves on."

" Well, I can tell you one thing," said A. B. junior, " if the Marquis of Dash had dropped his riding whip at Longley's feet, my young lord would have told one of his men to pick it up."

Some remark of this or another kind, concerning Rochefort, being made in Clara Belton's presence, that young lady flushing up considerably, retorted : " And if he is proud, he has something to be proud about. He is of far better family than we are, for instance, or than lots of the people he meets. Not that he is proud of that. . . . I don't believe him proud. . . . But if it is his pride which makes him generous and noble, as he is, and good and true as he is, I wish all men were a little prouder. I do not know anyone like my cousin ; I shall never know anyone like him again." She and Rochefort had become very well acquainted during the last two seasons, and she had always been his, and his wife's fast, firm friend.

When she heard of her cousin's great sorrow, she said she had a headache, and was going up-stairs to bathe her forehead. And when she was fastened into her room she lay down on her bed, with her face turned towards the pillows, and her hands clasped, and cried for two whole hours ; shedding the bitterest and the most heart-felt tears that were shed for him in England, and yet Lady Hallingford and some others shed tears that were painfully felt as well.

"Mamma is dreadfully put out about all this," said Mrs. Templeton to her sister, when she called and saw Clara alone for ten minutes ; "I suppose you know Lady Hallingford is leaving town at once, and in consequence, Lord Hallingford also ?"

"I should think she was," was Clara's brief remark.

"It is a great pity she has had to give up her morning concert. It was the day after to-morrow, wasn't it ? They say she is half out of her mind. By-the-bye, as I came along, I passed Sir Charles Glanville's house, quite shut up. Where are they gone to, do you know?"

"To his place in Scotland, mamma was told. Lady Glanville is so ill that they had to take her in an invalid carriage."

"She was so devotedly fond of Ernest, you see. And really, it's a very serious thing for them. I don't suppose, however, it is 'love to the death' or anything of that absurd kind with him. It is necessary he should marry and settle, you see, on account of the baronetcy."

"There's little Bernard at Harrow," interrupted Clara, rather bluntly, and scarcely looking at things from her sister's point of view.

Erminia was a good wife, and a good mother, but she had developed into a woman of the world (not having married after her heart) to "quick-march" time.

"Oh, well, yes; there's Bernard. But one does not consider him, of course. What did you mean by speaking of Bernard?"

"Only that I should think no woman worth anything, or with any feeling, would marry Ernest now," pursued Clara, with a somewhat flushed face. " I cannot imagine that any Englishwoman would put her hand into his."

"Oh, I don't know," returned her sister ; " it will blow over in time, as far as *he* is concerned. However, he has done a very shameful thing, and behaved very disgracefully," she added, " and it is a dreadful affair altogether. But really I must not keep baby waiting any longer, he is being driven up and down in the road."

She rose to go, and the sisters kissed each other.

" There! that reminds me," exclaimed Mrs. Templeton, " how foolish I am ! I was nearly going away without asking you something. Mamma is anxious to know, Clara (and she begged me to speak to you about it), if anything passed between you and Lord Hallingford the other night—the very night this unhappy affair took place.— Did there ? Has he said anything to you ?"

" If you mean did he make me an offer,"

answered Clara, colouring a little, "of course
I.can tell you—yes, he did."

" He proposed to you in proper form !"

" I really don't know whether it was in
proper form," returned her sister, almost
laughing, " because I have never been told
what the proper form is. But he proposed
to me."

" Well."

" Well ?"—

" Surely you are going to tell me something more ?"

" Yes, if you wish. I refused him ; and
I should be very glad if you would tell
mamma that I did. I would much rather
not speak to her myself about it."

" You positively refused Lord Hallingford ?"

" Yes.—But please don't tell anybody,
and ask mamma not to. I suppose you
must tell George, but say that I particularly
wish him not to speak of it. It would be in
wretched taste, and very ungenerous to Lord
Hallingford."

" Well, it would, rather ; for I must say
I think he has paid you more attention than

he has paid anyone else this season. If you had made up your mind not to have him, Clara, you ought to have let him see it, I think."

"I have tried, Minnie; but it was impossible to know exactly what he meant, till —till he spoke to me. You must tell mamma, to console her," continued Clara, "that I don't think he took my refusal much to heart; in fact, he seemed rather relieved than otherwise! I don't believe it is he who has wanted me at all; it is his mother who wanted him to marry me."

"Well, he has paid you a great compliment, at any rate."

"A great compliment, has he? I dare say he has; as I am so plain. Well, I hope he will get someone else, Minnie. I would go and be a housemaid before I would have him, that's all," said Clara, as she gave her sister her hand.

"You are a strange girl," said Mrs. Templeton; "I don't think you will ever marry. Well, tell mamma that I will come and see her this afternoon, about six o'clock. Goodbye."

She went downstairs to her carriage, cogitating many things in mind, but not sorry, perhaps, on the whole, that her younger and plainer sister was not to be made a countess of just yet!

" I will rest on the other side of the water," Rochefort had said to his doctor; but the rest did not come when it was sought.

He was scarcely in Antwerp before the fever of brain and nerve which had been dogging his every footstep during the last few days and nights—which had eaten and drank, risen up and laid down with him—which had followed him across the sea, never losing sight or touch for one moment of its prey—chose the moment at last for seizing him with an iron hand, flinging and laying him prostrate—prostrate in delirium, in sleeplessness, in burning fever, in despair, and utterly alone.

He had refused to take anyone with him. If he required a servant, he could get one, he said, in Brussels or Paris.

The hotel-keeper in terror sent for a doctor. The doctor brought a Sister of

Mercy, and sent off a telegram in haste to
Riverswood.   It was received when poor
Mrs. Longley was already ill in bed, and
threatened with a return of all her worst
symptoms, from the shock of Lady Hallingford's letter.   Rochefort had sent a note to
his aunt, asking her to write, and she wrote
beautifully; but no possible tenderness of
consideration could divest such news of its
shame and horror.

"Everyone in London feels for, and sym-
pathises with your son," wrote the countess.
" He has gained but one opinion among all
those who knew him.   For myself, I dare
not think what I have lost.   No amount of
gaiety and distraction (and it has been one
of the gayest, and what I call 'hardest,'
seasons I have known for years) has prevented his being always ready with his co-
operation, his sympathy, his clear, thoughtful
sense, to help and to encourage me in all
the work which you know I cut out for
myself years ago in London, and which
increases and widens constantly.   He was
only too generous—often I would not let him

give when he wanted to, because I knew what immense sums must be going in one way and another, especially with poor Mrs. Rochefort's extravagant tastes, and almost reckless indulgence of her fancies. He was so fond of her that he could not bear to hear her called extravagant, and said he did not think her so. She was very, very beautiful; and she has been exceedingly " run after" and admired, but I wish he had never brought her from the country! Rochefort is going abroad, and says he will write to you from Antwerp or Brussels. Don't let him stay abroad too long. Persuade him to come back—if it is only to go away again—that he may not lose the sense of all the active, healthy, and full life that is still waiting for him in England, if he will take it up. His is too fine a life, with too much prospect before it, to be wasted on regrets and morbid sentiment."

In spite of the strong infusion of wholesome iron tonic mixed in the cup which it was Lady Hallingford's unenviable task to present in the shape of this letter, it

had struck poor Mrs. Longley to the earth.
She was seriously ill with grief, indignation,
and anxiety about her son, when the Antwerp telegram sent fresh consternation
through the household. Mrs. Robinson took
counsel with the butler, and they decided
to open it, before taking it to the mistress.

" Lord have mercy! what's to be done
now?" inquired Mortimer, sitting down, and
changing from pale to red, and red to pale.
" It'll never do to tell the missus."

" It would be the death of her. I wish
the doctor were here."

" When is he coming again?" asked the
butler.

" He isn't coming again till to-morrow
morning. Do you know what I think, Mr.
Mortimer ? We ought to get Mary Rudge
to go," said the housekeeper.

" Go to Antwerp ?"

" Yes, to Antwerp ; and you will have to
take her, and stay as long as the master's
ill. He oughtn't to be alone, I'm sure."

" Well, I don't mind," said the butler,
rather restored by the feeling of importance

this sudden suggestion gave to him. "I might as well go as another; and some one must go, it's certain."

"Send one of the men to the lodge at once, then!" exclaimed the housekeeper, "and I will order the horses to be got ready. If she's quick, you can catch the afternoon train up."

"How about old Stephen, though?" inquired the butler, with a momentary qualm of doubt.

"Say he shall come up here, and we'll take care of him. He can have one of Mary's nieces to attend to him; he's used to Sally. Tell William to say so. Send William, because he can run. Stop—I'll go and speak to him; for she must get packed up this moment. There's not any time to be lost."

Would Mary go to him? Yes, God knew she would—anywhere over the earth! Was he very ill? When should they get there? Where was the cord of her box? "Steph, your new shirt is in that drawer at the right-hand side." Who would go for Sally? " William, tell them to air his sheets well, or he'll catch his death." When would the phaeton be here? She was nearly ready. "Help me to fold this shawl, William," and would he be sure and stay with her husband till Sally came? Where was her umbrella? There—she was ready now, and, " Oh, good gracious, why doesn't the carriage come?" She thought she had only twenty minutes, and—there it was! How the horses tore! "Good-bye, Steph; God bless you! Keep up till I'm back. I'm ready, Mr. Mortimer. Oh, Mortimer, shall we catch the train?" And then, as they drove along, the poor woman had her cry out—the cry she had stifled back so bravely, as long as there was any work for her to do.

" Did the telegram say he was very bad?" she inquired, when she could command her voice to speak, and looking up with tear-stained cheeks.

" It isn't a nice telegram," said the butler; " this is what it is," and he pulled it out of his pocket and read it to her.

Mary could say no more, she kept silence the rest of the way to Gowerford, struggling bravely to subdue her emotion, and to think hopefully.

" Perhaps when he sees a face from home it will give him the right turn," she said to herself, and sustained herself by that hope.

When they arrived at the Hôtel St. Antoine in Antwerp, the hotel-keeper, who was summoned at once to see them, said he could not let any one into Mr. Longley's room without permission from the doctor. Those were the doctor's own orders, even should it be Mr. Longley's mother herself. "When would the doctor be there again?" "He came three times a-day; he would be here in an hour. In the meantime the gentleman wanted nothing; 'la Sœur' was with him. Would not monsieur and madame like a little refreshment after their long journey?" Mortimer having intimated to the Swiss waiter, "who talked English," and through whose good offices this little dialogue had been conducted, that they were greatly in need of refreshment ; a first-rate repast was served up to them, of which Mary ate but very little, and of which the butler ate a great deal, saying to Mrs. Robinson afterwards, that " he had never enjoyed any food half so much in his life, and that they know how to manage things in these foreign hotels, and no mistake !"

When the doctor came, the obliging little Swiss waiter was again in requisition. This good lady, then, was a nurse sent by the mother of the English gentleman, ill up-stairs ? Very good. But he (the doctor) must demand that the sister of mercy should also remain for the present, as she was now *au fait* of the case, and, probably, also the good lady, whom Madame la mère de monsieur had done him the honour of sending to his assistance, would be unable to understand his French, as he, on his side, would be unable to understand her English.

Mary would not interfere in any way with the " sister ;" she would do anything she was told, if only she might see the gentleman, and attend on him.

Certainly ; à l'instant ; but she must not speak, or make a sound. She might take the place of the " sister," in laying the wet cloths on his head ; gradually, she might speak to him, arrange his pillows, and so on ; but she must be very cautious. The least excitement was dangerous ; the case was already one of great danger. Did she thoroughly understand her instructions ? She must pardon these endless cautions. Monsieur had not slept for several days and nights. He passed from delirium to stupor, and from stupor to delirium. Almost every sound was intolerable to him.

" I didn't know," said Mortimer to himself when he was left alone in the coffee-room, " I didn't know there were such knowing doctors out of England. That chap beats all I've seen hollow, for carefulness. Good-looking fellow, too. Hope he'll bring the master round—by George ! I do."

Mary was taken up many flights of stairs to a suite of rooms nearly at the top of the

hotel. Here they had had to move Rochefort that he might be the more out of the
way of noise. Nearly the whole flat had
been abandoned to him, for before he had
become delirious, he had said to the doctor,
" Save my life, if you can, for my mother's
sake. Money is no object to me. I have
enough for everything ;" and then he had
written for him—hardly able to guide his
hand—the address of his English home.

When his foster-mother entered the large
dimly-lighted room, she saw the black figure
of the good Catholic sister of mercy, slightly
bending over a prostrate, motionless form,
as she laid the wetted linen cloths upon the
brow and head. All his hair was gone ;
Mary did not know her boy and her master,
as she knelt by him and gazed in terror upon
his face. Good God !—could *this* be him ?

When the doctor left, he said in a low voice
to the sister, " There will be plenty of work
for the two of you, I see. We should have
had to get another nurse, any way."

" It is as well they cannot understand
each other," he reflected, as he went down-

stairs, " then there will be no talking. I wonder how they will get on. But Marie Angélique would get on with the fiend himself, so I don't suppose she'll quarrel with a nice-looking Englishwoman."

Once and only once during the next few hours did Mary transgress a little the doctor's orders. Rochefort opened his eyes and looked at her : it was only for a moment, but theñ he moved the hand, which was flung out hot and white upon the sheet, a little way towards her, the palm upwards, as if wishing to clasp hers. She gave him her hand, and held his close.

" Is it——" He was either too exhausted to utter the word " Mary," or his mind was again wandering.

She stooped down, forcing back the tears which had rushed to her eyes at the first sound of his altered voice, and said—

" It is your own old nurse, my darling. And you will get quite well now. Only don't speak."

The sister of mercy held a warning finger to her lips, and shook her head ; but she did both with a kind smile.

And these two, during long, fearful days
of exhaustion or delirium, and through
sleepless, agonized nights, when the brain
of the sufferer was like one open nerve,
exposed and sensitive to every faintest
word, to every most distant sound; while
the cruel, unrelenting July sun baked
those outer walls, and heated, in spite of
every appliance art could devise, the air
of that chamber, in which one breath of
cool air would have been treasured as a
gift from heaven ; these two—now fearing,
now hoping, now despairing—fought, with
the good physician at their side, a brave
hand - to - hand fight with death. With
unwearied patience they struggled to re-
gain every inch of ground they had
to yield—though they might again yield
every inch they had regained ! — were
incessantly watchful, unremittingly on
guard ; resolute and faithful in their de-
fence of the life-citadel committed to their
charge.

Would God hear their prayers (for they
did pray, each after her own fashion) ; or

had the time come when the last step in
life's journey had been taken, and when
the young traveller and the hopeful worker
must travel and must work no more, arrested
in his path by the Divine Hand, before whose
shadow the strongest and the best must
faint and fall?

*   *   *   *

CHAPTER VII.

WHEN Nora left her husband's home she hurried on foot, and by ways she hardly knew, to an hotel of which she remembered the name, and where she knew there was no faint chance of her being recognized. Here she wrote the note which was delivered to Mr. Glanville as he was cooling himself in one of the refreshment rooms at Mrs. Cavendish's, after a dance. Those who saw it given him, saw him first tear it open with his usual air of easy coolness; then glance through it, his face first flushing crimson, and then becoming deadly white; saw him thrust it into his pocket, and go out of the room without a word.

" Singular," said one of the gentlemen,

when some ladies who were present had moved away with their attendant cavaliers, laughing and talking, "wasn't it?"

"Summons of a romantic nature, I should imagine," laughed a second; "Glanville has generally a one-volume novel in action, I believe, though not in the press."

"Bedford Hotel," said Mr. Glanville, springing into the first cab he saw empty, when he was out in the street, "and drive for your life!"

Nora was walking up and down the floor of the upper room into which she had been shown, when she heard his step upon the stairs, and turning as he opened the door, faced him.

"Have you just sent me this?" inquired Ernest, pale to the very lips, as he came up to her and opened the note he had just received before her eyes.

She glanced at it, pushed it slightly back towards him, and said, in a trembling voice—

"Yes, I sent it; and I am here now for you to answer it."

There was a moment's dead pause.

" What has he seen ?   What does he know ?" asked Ernest.

" He has seen your letters."

"My letters?" It is impossible to describe the tone with which he said it.

" He unlocked one of my jewel-cases, and found them, and read them."

"And why,—why in the name of all that's infernal, Nora, did you keep my letters ?"

There was no answer.

" Nora, why did you keep my letters ?"

After a few minutes, she answered, in an altered voice, and with tears gathering in her eyes, which, however, she tried to force back—

" Because I loved you, and I thought you loved me. I could not bear to tear them, till I had had them a little. I see now what a fool I have been—every way !"

Ernest took one or two rapid turns in the room, struggling with an awful sensation in his throat, and in his heart, that seemed as if it would suffocate him. At last he stopped before her.

"You know that I love you. You know I have loved you too well. But my God! . . . . I never meant it should come to this!"

(What man who sins ever does "mean it should come to this"?)

"Has Rochefort sent you away from him?" he inquired, after a minute's pause.

"No, I have run away. He was terribly, terribly angry, and I could not stay with him. No one knows where I am."

"For God's sake, then, Nora, before it is too late, go back! Every moment you are here makes things worse. You know how he loves you. He would forgive you even now. Don't, don't, for pity's sake, let this get all over London. In two hours, in one hour, we are ruined; I—you—your husband—all three of us! It is absolute madness for you to stay here."

Nora, who had sat down when he began to speak, looked at him as if she were gradually awaking from a dream to some horrible reality. She could scarcely believe it was Ernest who spoke to her. At last she rose, saying, with a forced calm—

"Thank you, Mr. Glanville. . . . You have introduced me, for the first time, to the gentleman for whom I have betrayed my husband. I am infinitely obliged to you ;" and with a bend of mock ceremony, though her face was ashy white, she moved towards the door.

"What are you going to do?" said Ernest, putting himself against it, and holding the lock with his hand.

"That is of no moment to you, sir. I can leave you if I like, I suppose ? And I choose to leave you," she added, stamping her foot. "Let me go."

"You cannot go unless I allow you. Take your hand off, Nora !—you know that all your strength will not move one of my fingers. What did you mean by what you said to me just now ?"

"I mean that I have loved a man who does not love me. That I am the unhappiest and the most wretched of women."

"You are making me the most wretched of men."

"Yes, because I tell you you have been found out !"

"Do you know what you are saying?" exclaimed her lover, almost fiercely. "Do you wish to insult me?—I only want," he went on in excessive agitation—"I only want to screen and to protect you from infamy that will be enough to kill you—infamy of which at this moment, you realize—you know—you think nothing! And for that you taunt me, as if I had no manliness left in me—as if I were a dastardly coward—a shameless sneak! Have I not loved you when I have risked my whole future for you? Do I not love you now as passionately as ever—now at this moment, though I am begging you to leave me?"

The poor girl looked up at him; looked —and then threw herself upon his breast.

"Why do you ask me to leave you, then, when I have nowhere on earth to go to?"

"My darling—it was of your own will you came to me. Your husband has not cast you off. . . . But you are making it more and more impossible to return to him, every moment you are with me. Do not you see you are?"

"You can send me away," she said, forcing herself loose from him, " and I will go. But not back to my husband ; you have not made me bad enough for that, bad as you have made me."

" Are you mad, Nora ? Where would you go ?"

"God knows. You do not care !"—

" I do care."

" Why do you speak so to me, then ?" she said, bursting into tears at last. " You are breaking my heart."

"What do you want me to do, Nora ?"

" To do ?—I want you to protect me in some way, that I may not suffer the shame of being under my husband's protection."

" But will it not be far worse shame to be under mine ?" he asked.

" I don't want to see you, or to be near you. I don't want to be any trouble to you, but I will not be indebted for the bread I eat, and the roof that shelters me, to him. I shall never forget his look of anger—of hatred. He hates me now, and he hates you !"

" You do not blame him for that, do you? Do you think I should not hate him, if he had done what I have ? If I had known he would ever find out how I had injured him, I would have stood up to be shot, before I spoke one word of love to you, Nora !"

" Do you mean that ?" she asked.

" I mean it as truly as there is a God in heaven."

"Ernest . . . . did you not tell me again and again that it was not wrong to love you ? You told it me so often and with such ——" here her voice broke for a moment, and she could not go on. "You told it me so often, that I almost believed you at last. Have you forgotten all you said?"

Forgotten ? No, God knew he had not forgotten ! He was not likely to forget now.

" You have been wickedly — wickedly cruel to me !" she burst out in uncontrollable grief. " You had plenty of words then ; you have not one word to comfort me now !—I wish I had never seen you !— Oh God, I wish I had died when I was a little innocent child !"

He knelt beside her—he kissed her ; he

dried her eyes, he said what he could to comfort her, but his words were impotent now ; his caresses were like the sting of thorns about her ; his kisses were drained of all their sweetness, all their balm, for the evil he had, inflicted. She was desolate with his voice in her ears : she felt unloved with her lover before her.

When she was a little calmer Ernest said, " Nora, you told me just now that your husband hated you, and that is why you will not go back to him. It would be easy for me to save you from his hatred—I could do it by writing half a dozen lines. Would you like me to write them ?" She raised her eyes and looked at him.

" And say what is not true, I suppose ?"

" What is very pardonable untruth, if it is untruth at all. You do not suppose I am brute enough to reproach you for anything that has happened, do you ?"

" He would not look at anything you wrote, Ernest, or read it, or believe it.— What is the use ?"

" He would, if I sent it through Sidney.

I will write to Sidney now :—let me do it,
Nora!—matters can be no worse—and they
may be made better; for you at least."

"Yes, by making yourself out the greatest
villain that walks the earth.—Is that it ?"

" Well—it is what I have been. Rochefort cannot detest me more than he does.
It is of little consequence what he thinks of
me now. And it is of incalculable importance what he thinks of you."

Nora sat for some minutes, with her hands
clasped before her on her lap, and thought.

" Well," she said at last, " you may write
if you like, and if you think it will do any
good."

He rang the bell, ordered pen, ink, and
paper, and sat down. She let him write
for several minutes—beginning first one
sheet and then another, without interrup-
tion, and watching him as he did so. Then
all at once, starting up, she said—

" Give me that paper, Ernest. It is utterly useless, and worse than useless. Do
you think he will believe I have not cared
for you ? And, after all, can you possibly

say anything to justify me ? You know you cannot—nothing that will justify me to him." As Ernest stopped writing, but held his hand between her and the paper, that she might not reach it, she added—

"He would have died I believe before he would have been unfaithful to me. Where is your chance of making any excuse for me ?"

"Do you mean that Rochefort has been always and entirely faithful to you ? How can you be sure of it ?"

"I am sure, perfectly sure. And you are sure too. You know him well enough."

Glanville pushed away the papers from before him, leaned his arms on the table, and then his head on his hands. Nora heard him groan several times like a man in insufferable pain. At last, he got up, and began pacing the room, without ever looking at, or speaking to her.

She bore his silence till she could bear it no more, and till she felt it was an insult.

"Mr. Glanville," she began, " have you said all you have to say to me ? If you

have, I may leave you I suppose? I have
been ready to leave you some time."

"You shall not go till you tell me where
you are going," he answered, almost bluntly.

"Where I am going?" she repeated,
lashed up to sudden, and almost savage
anger; "where? Into the streets — into
the river—anywhere. Going to kill myself, perhaps. What is it to you? What
is it to anyone? You have ruined—ruined
—ruined me," she reiterated, with a frantic
stamp of her foot at each word; "and I
hate you—loathe you—and . . . . .
open that door and let me out, I tell you!"
He caught her in his arms, as she laughed
in his face; laughed—and laughed again;
and then fell back with shrieking sobs.

He stayed with her for the next hour;
he stayed till she was restored; and till all
that could be done for her, was done. When
he heard that she had fallen asleep, exhausted by the long violence of her agitation,
he wrote a hurried note, to be given to her
when she awoke, left her in the best care

he could, and went off to the ———— Hotel,
for the rest of the night.

Before morning, he had had ample time
for reflection : and he reflected after this
wise. The doors of his home were now
closed to him : the doors of society were
closed to him ; it was not in the power of
himself—of Rochefort—of anyone, to prevent the story of his villainy, or of the disgrace of the woman he had loved, from
spreading like contagion over London—over
England, nay, farther and wider than that,
for it would be known wherever English
newspapers were read. His future lay a
blank before him ; his present—where was
his present ? Where could he go ? What
house was open to him ? What hand would
meet his in friendship, or even in pity ?
He had snatched at exquisite and forbidden
fruit, but it was at least his own now; though
stolen by shameless treachery. It lay at
his feet still, and he would stoop, and take
it up, and keep it ; since he had been
almost asked to do so! Therefore, not because
his passion irresistibly impelled him, not

because his infatuation was now beyond his
control, not because he was blind to consequences, or deaf to an inner, warning voice
which told him he might have to pay in
heavy coin for this second lapse from right,
—but because he saw nothing else to do—
he did what he was almost driven to do,
hating the deed, and hating himself.

And this was "the romance" of Mrs.
Rochefort Longley's elopement.

We must do Ernest the poor justice of
saying that he was miserably sorry it had
been his fate to injure Rochefort, of all men
on this earth. He would never have quite
forgiven himself, had his fault not "found
him out;" but as it was, he would have
suffered a great deal to undo what was now
done for evermore. He was not a naturally
bad man, he was not hardened in any sin ;
he had had (until now) a certain code of
honour, common to himself and to men like
him ; and this was the first time he had
overstepped it. He had not overstepped it
deliberately, or in cool blood :—he had done

what so many have done, nourished a strong
fancy till it became a passion ; then thrown
the reins on its neck ; let it career headlong
with him, till his brain reeled, and his
heart was on fire ; when at last, the pre-
cipice was in front of him, had—or believed
he had—no power to put on curb, or to
draw bridle ; and woke from the delirium
into which the want of all honourable and
manly self-control had thrown him, to find
he had acted the part of traitor to his
friend, and of villain to the woman whose
love had made her weak.

Whose love had made her weak ! Oh,
chivalry of old, and simple, and heroic
days ! how we want you back in this
England of the nineteenth century ! When
will some hand, mighty and unfaltering in
its power ; some heart, courageous in its
pure, proud love of woman—raise a banner
at whose sight the "sons of God shall sing
together for joy ;"—a banner of white—
for Purity ; of gold—for Divinity ; and
around which shall gather, all who in God's
name, shall vow to fight with shield and

sword, against the foul fiend of iniquity ; who, armed with prayer, and helmeted with strength, shall first subdue " the sin that is within them," and then fight the good fight of faith, unto the last, against "all such lusts as war against the soul," and flesh of man !

Oh, St. Alfred of old ! bravest, tenderest, most heroic; most Christian, and most truly chivalrous of kings !—thou, who on a cold church's cold, unfeeling floor, day by day, and night by night—in thy hot and passionate youth—didst pray God to afflict thee with any pain, rather than let thy nature fall below the height to which thy wish and prayer would raise it ! — and who, afterwards, through long years, didst suffer with the fortitude of thy Master—though with "sweat as of blood upon the brow," —the stern and Divine answer to that purest prayer e'er raised on earth ; oh, St. Alfred ! has thy great heart descended to no one among thy Saxon English, that we may look onward to the day when true chivalry shall be preached afresh ; but with power such as it never wielded yet, because the need is greater!—with blast of its pure trumpet, such as has never yet been blown —except the Lord blew—and let us pray Him to blow it now!

We pray for many things ; for heat, for rain, for prosperity, for health, for life ; let us join hands, and pray with bowed heads, and in sackcloth and ashes, for the reign of Christian purity on earth!

CHAPTER VIII.

WE believe it is usual with novel writers (or, at least, with English ones) to draw a becoming, and almost closed, veil over the proceedings, wanderings, sayings, and doings of lovers who have no right to be lovers : of a man, for instance, who has run away with his friend's wife, and a wife who has chosen to desert her husband.

This custom, however, it is not our present intention to follow. We intend to present a very tame picture, in very tame, and we trust, by no means fascinating colours ; giving a fair idea of the amount of happiness gained by a dereliction of duty, so absolutely ruinous to the fair fame and the worldly prospects and position (to say nothing more) of one at least of the parties concerned in it, that nothing short of a state of "seventh heaven" could by any possibility compensate in the least degree for all that is irretrievably lost !

Where were they to go ? Italy and Switzerland were—or very soon would be— over-run with English and Americans. Every place where there was life ; where there were distractions ; where there was any cool air from lake or mountain ; where there were baths for refreshment, and mineral waters to drink ; where the sea-breezes brought, morning and evening, their delicious and reviving tonic to expectant and exhausted hundreds ;—all these places the two of whom we write were compelled to shun, as they would shun the pest. They, of all others, who most needed the distraction of constant change and constant company, to make the present tolerable, to drug the memory of the past, and to prevent the mind from dwelling with too painful an anxiety on what the future might have in store, were driven to each other, as almost their only resource ; were forced to find in the companionship which had been their bane, and which, in its guilt, separated them "as by a great gulf" from all other friendship or sympathy, their only refuge from ennui, the only poor consolation for their solitude and their exile.

Of the two, Glanville felt the monotony and the aimlessness of their daily life the most. Nora had still this to carry her through her shame,—that she was passionately fond of him ; that his very presence, his voice, his slightest caress, his glance, his manner, his way of talking to her, everything about him, retained still its old and fatal fascination. She had never really loved her husband ; but this man she loved as much as it was in her power to love any one.

Ernest had no real affection for the woman he had ruined. He had had a passion for her ; and he regarded her now with a mixture of tenderness and pity, tinctured with a very slight feeling of contempt.

His nature was more complex than hers ;

he had a keener perception, and a stronger appreciation of what was in itself right and good, than she ; and he fell more lamentably and shamefully below his standard.   He asked more from life and from friendship than she did ; he believed in more (in a certain sense, that is), and felt more ; and yet she was entirely incapable of the recklessness, the seeming insincerities, the changes of feeling, the inconsistencies in act and speech, the fitful homage to good, and the deep lapses into evil, which went to make up Ernest's character and life, and which make up the character and life of so many like him.

*   *   *   *

A few days after leaving England, a lady and gentleman, under an assumed name, took "un appartement" on the second floor of a house in the grand and quiet "Cours Moraud" in Lyons.   Here they would see no English, unless they went to the little English church on Sunday mornings ; an event which was scarcely likely to occur.

In this Cours Moraud they felt hidden,

and were hidden, from the eyes of the world. There was nothing to be done, but to pace in the early mornings and in the cool of the short evenings, up and down the Boulevard under the trees, or to walk along the broad quays, and through the high, sombre, massive-built streets, or to sit and eat ices in the cafés, cool with their dark green Venetians and striped awnings, and beautiful with flowering pots of magnolia before the doors, and cool mirrors, white marble tables, and tiny splashing fountains.

Sometimes they went excursions on the river, sometimes drove into the country ; but Ernest liked best sauntering along the streets with the poor, beautiful girl, whom he called " sa femme," leaning on his arm. He liked to fancy that the passers-by admired her, and gave him credit for being " un mari Anglais dévot." When he was in the midst of other men, each and all of whom he believed to be no better, and often much worse, than himself, he did not feel so vile—when in the midst of trees, and fields, and vineyards, he hated and despised himself.

The occupations of walking or driving out filled the two ends of the day, or sometimes only one. There were then the remaining seven, eight, or nine hours to be disposed of. Letters were demanded by, and would have been welcomed by, no one. They could not converse without being in constant danger of bringing up subjects, or reverting to scenes, of which they dared not speak or think in each other's presence. There was scarcely a human being whose name they might introduce into conversation without the possibility, or the certainty, of its suggesting an idea or a memory that would cause pain to both. Nora had little taste for reading, and tired of the occupation in an hour. It was too hot to work, and she was too listless to play, unless Ernest chose to sing.

He did not very often care to sing. Nora was not equal to many of his accompaniments, and he accompanied himself badly, never having been used to play for his own songs. He was very amiable (when he saw she was really and badly in want of occupation), in letting her try what she could do, and helping her with suggestions and explanations; but the music-lessons generally ended in her saying, with a sigh, "How I wish I could play for you like Harriet!" (Harriet being the name of his eldest and married sister), and in Ernest's replying "Yes; there's a good deal in the accompaniment being played right, isn't there?" After which he would throw himself on the sofa, light a cigar, and either take up his novel, or try and go to sleep.

After being accustomed—as they both were—to large rooms, plenty of space; beautiful surroundings of all sorts; horses, carriages, perfect attendance; free air, and indefinite liberty at all times, the position of being cooped up in one small "salon," looking on to a quiet French boulevard (and even this shut out from them during a great part of the day, by the necessity of keeping the Venetian shutters closed), in a strange town, where they did not know a soul; with no amusement but that of an occasional visit to the theatre in the evening, and with one "bonne" to wait on them, who brought up the coffee in a morning, dressed in a dingy petticoat and a dingy grey jacket, and who did not always present the glasses and silver at dinner in a state of absolute perfection; under these circumstances their position was not enviable. Sometimes it was very nearly intolerable. It would have been easy to go into Switzerland; but anywhere in Switzerland they might now meet anybody. They could not be certain, wherever they went, of not seeing Rochefort himself. They knew he was not in England. Ernest had written a short note to Sidney from Paris; and Sidney had replied by a few sorrowful lines, at the end of which he stated the fact of Nora's husband being abroad, but he did not know where. Ernest's dread of meeting him, by some horrible chance, grew to have the force of a presentiment in his mind—it pursued him like a nightmare— he dare not move. This worst and most trying complication of his already very unenviable circumstances he had never once calculated on having to endure.

One day, in desperation at the length of
the hours between déjeûner at twelve o'clock
and dinner at half-past six, Ernest wrote a
long letter to his brother. He was in an
unhappy humour when he wrote it, though
the evening before he had been in unna-
turally high spirits, and had talked nonsense, and mimicked the actors they had
seen in a light comedy at the theatre, till
Nora thought he was going wild.

It was a letter full of contradictions in
feeling. He began in a careless, almost
flippant style ; then broke suddenly into
bitter self-accusation, and bitterer regrets,
which made poor Sidney's heart ache for
him as he read. Then his tone became
indifferent ; then despairing ; and, lastly,
sad.

He could not help himself, he said ; he
had not been made or created to struggle
against temptation. Why had fate thrown
such a woman in his way ? After all, it
was the sin against his friend that made
him the sinner he was ; otherwise he was
not worse than many another man, against

whom society had pronounced no ban. If
he had thought for a moment Rochefort
would ever discover the injury he had done
him, he would have been hung before he
would have done it. Now, the devil only
knew what was to become of himself, and
Nora. He could not pass his life in hiding
in first one foreign town and then another.
And then money comes to an end some-
time. It had not been very easy to raise
the money he had brought with him, or
arranged to draw for. If he had occasion
for more, would Sidney lend it him? It
was so deucedly ruinous getting it from
those Jew brokers; and he supposed the
governor wouldn't fork out anything, while
he was abroad in this position. Of course
he would repay Sidney everything when
he had his mother's fortune. He did not
forget that he owed him too much already.
If his brother could make any suggestion
to him, or give him any advice which it
would be possible to follow, he should be
devoutly thankful. He wished, of course,
to behave in all honour to poor Nora; but

what the deuce was he to do with her?
It was a great pity that she did not happen
to be a Roman Catholic. In that case he
might, possibly, persuade her to enter a
convent at the end of a year or so, perhaps
sooner. All the French women who got
themselves into bad scrapes, and had a
little religion, entered convents. He didn't
think Protestantism had been an unalloyed
good, by any means, &c., &c., &c. How was
his mother? How was poor Augusta?—
He could not bear to think of Augusta.
He only hoped to Heaven she was too
young and too innocent to know how far
her brother had fallen. He supposed Bernard knew all about it. "For God's sake,
Sid, don't let him think me as bad as I
am, if you can help it. Poor little chap!
he thought so much of me, and was always
trying 'to come up to me,' as he said.
Perhaps the boys at Harrow will point
him out now to the new ones, and say,
'That's the fellow whose brother——' I
can't bear to think of it, Sidney! * *
* * * * *

Perhaps I am exaggerating everything in my mind—but what with dwelling on things, and not having any fellow to talk to me—I don't know what I'm coming to. I know you will all miss me; and Bernard will wonder what he's to do without me when he comes home for the holidays. I say, Sid, will you give him my two riding-whips (they are hanging in my room), and tell him to take care of the best one; and give him my dear love; and tell him we'll live to be friends, and to see each other again yet? You don't suppose there's any chance he won't know what I'm away for, do you? If it had been a year or two ago —but you see he's fifteen now, and fellows are sure to tell him. I saw the whole thing in the *Galignani* myself, when we first got here. I dared not think of the river for two days after. I don't like to go too near it now, sometimes. *The dulness is awful.* Tell mother I hope and pray she will get well, and not worry herself about me, if she can help; but I dare not begin sending messages to mother; I will write to her

some day, perhaps. I wish she would write
to me first. I don't mind how much she
blows me up; it would do me good to be
rated and raved at. * * *
* * * Has the governor sold
my horse and cab ? If he has, I wish you
would get the money for me, and send it
me. When you get' back to Brookwood, I
want you to make Lindsay bring you all
the books—French and otherwise—out of
my room ; and when you have an hour to
spare, look them over, and pitch all the
rubbish into the fire. If you don't, Bernard will get at them, and they wouldn't
all do him good. I daresay he reads—or
will read—trashy, vile stuff sometimes ;
but I don't want to have any hand in it if
he does. Tell him to be kind to the dogs,
poor fellows ! and take them out with him—
how they will miss me this shooting-season ;
I shall miss them, I know. Poor Augusta !
she will have no one to ride out with her,
but Bernard. Tell Bernard to remember
how I told him to manage Lady Jane, if
she reared. I'm not quite sure that he

ought to ride Lady Jane ; she's not a perfect temper, and she's rather hard mouthed.
I don't want to hear of the little chap
coming. to grief; and he's very fearless.
(Don't forget about the whips ; he hadn't a
nice whip last holidays, and wanted one,
but he'd spent all his money.) I often
think he'll be baronet, after all, Sid. If
anything happens, that I don't come back
to England—or if I should be driven, by
having nothing else to do, to make an end
of myself; or if I die 'a natural death' (I
hope you think I'm ending this letter with
decency and propriety—I feel it is quite
solemn myself), try and talk to him a bit
sometimes, and save him from being what
I am.—Oh, Sidney! dear old boy! I wish
I were having a talk to you, in the old
room at home, looking down through the
oak trees on to the river, and smoking my
pipe. I wonder if you are being grilled,
as we are! There is no green here anywhere; but there never is any green like
the English green.—Try and forgive me, or
else pity me, and write me a long letter.

I am utterly wretched at times. We shall be obliged to leave here, and travel; that is if I can get hold of a little more money, but I am so awfully possessed by the fear I told you of, that I cannot make up my mind where to go. Of course I know it's an entirely morbid fear—at least, to the extent I have it—and very ridiculous; but my mind is altogether unstrung and morbid at present. I shall fix on some place to go to in *Spain*, I think, or else in California, or, perhaps, one of the Pacific islands would be as good a place as another! Don't laugh at me; I must do something to arrest the feeling, which is becoming stronger in my mind every day, that *dinner is the only thing on earth worth living for!*"

"What an immensely long letter you have written, Ernest," said Nora, putting down her book, and leaning wearily back on her chair, with her hands clasped over her head; "what on earth have you had to say?"

Glanville had the tears in his eyes, and

did not answer her at once, but got up and leaned with his arms against the mantel-piece.

" Ernest, what have you been saying?"

" Oh, I had a lot of things I wanted to say—about Bernard—and my horse and dogs—and money matters, and so on. Nora, should you mind my leaving you for half an hour for a turn on the quay? I'll be back in dinner time, and take you out a drive afterwards."

CHAPTER IX.

JUST at the end of August, "Madame Osborne," the young English lady living with her "husband" on the second flat of the house in the "Cours Moraud," was taken with a sharp attack, first of cold, and then of low fever. A doctor was sent for, and the doctor, after examining her lungs, informed "Monsieur" that they were in a very weak state, and that "sa femme" would require great care for some time. Ernest was completely *bouleversé* by this announcement. He did everything he could for her; he hired a maid to wait upon and nurse her; he gave her her medicines with his own hand; he went out and bought her beautiful flowers; fanned her; read to her, and, finally, when she was pronounced convalescent and able to go out, took her short, easy drives along the quays and boulevards, carrying her up and down the long stone staircase in his strong arms.

" Do not I tire you ?" she asked one day, as he laid her back on her sofa. " I could walk quite easily now."

" No, you do not tire me," he answered sadly, as he touched her cheek slightly with his hand; " you never tire me. I wish you did. The doctor wants me to take you to Plombières, Nora."

" But you will not do it ?" she exclaimed hurriedly; "there are so many people there! Let us go a little into the country, and then, when I am quite strong again, we can go into Austria, as we intended."

Ernest hired a small, light carriage, with horse and driver ; and together they set off into the hill country for a few weeks, in their search for health, if not for happiness.

The country they traversed, to minds at rest and undiseased, would have appeared almost perfect in its loveliness. Wherever,

from one of the hill-tops, or from the wind-
ing hill-roads which skirted delicious vineyards, and apple orchards, was seen in the
plain below, a broad glimpse of one of the
sister rivers, the Rhone or the Saone, the
scene was beyond utterance lovely, varied,
soft : rich in purple and rose lights ; in con-
trast of sun and shade; of meadow and forest;
of ravine and vineyard, and folded hills.

In one little village with red roofs to the
houses, with an old inn and an older church,
and approached by a steep ascent from the
high road, along which one great, rumbling
old diligence rolled every morning on its
way to Lyons, and every evening back; they
dismissed the carriage for a time, and took
up their abode at the inn. Every morning
they climbed one of the hill-sides, and sat
for hours under the shade of the trees—
the exquisite view, beautiful as a land
of dreams, spread out before :—Nora, on
her couch of shawls, with one of her
"Tauchnitz" books in her hand, and Ernest
lying full-length, with his *Galignani*, or
French novel, and smoking endless cigars.

It would have been Elysium if they had
been happy; if they had felt they had
the shadow of a right to be together ; as it
was they were almost miserable.

After dinner the evening would close in
quickly ; and then night, like a sudden veil
thrown over the earth, covered village and
mountain, forest and valley ; and the moon
would rise—queen regnant of the earth—
in pale, calm, holy state, and matchless
loveliness !

Ernest used to go into the inn-kitchen in
the evening ; smoke with the landlord and
the few farmers and soldiers, who would
come to sit by the great fire-place, and
smoke, talk, and sometimes sing. He soon
became a great favourite in the circle,—he
practised his French, and listened to their
patois; laughed and drank with them, and
learnt to enjoy these strange evenings more
than he would have thought it possible a
short time ago, when almost every drawing-
room in London was open to him.

One night, it happened that he wanted
a fresh case of cigars, or some such thing,

and sprang up the rickety stairs to his room in search of them, humming the refrain of a little French chanson as he went. When he was on the point of descending, he fancied he heard a smothered sound of sobbing, and stopped still to listen. Then he turned back and went to Nora's side.

" Are you there, Ernest?" she said.

" Yes, I am here. What in God's name is the matter? Don't frighten me so."

" It's the moonlight, Ernest! It shines so full and strong into the room. I cannot sleep."

" I will tell Madame Berger, and she shall send you something soothing. You have been overtired to-day. Will you have some eau de fleur d'oranger before I go down?"

" No, no; it isn't that," she answered. " I'm not tired."

" What is it, then? Tell me."

" Are you sure you won't mind?"

" Of course not. Tell me anything that troubles you."

She raised herself in bed, and putting her arms round his neck, and drawing his head near to hers, said,

"I was thinking of God, Ernest."

He was silent for a long time.

"Ernest, you know I have been very ill, and I am not very strong now, though I am so much better. Suppose I had to die? I think of it sometimes; I cannot help."

"Do not think about it; you are getting much better, indeed, quite well. You will soon be just what you were. Look here— let me go down and get you something, you are exhausted. Will you have some champagne if I bring it you? You had hardly any dinner."

"Ernest, do be a little bit serious for once! I can't tell you how unhappy I am sometimes. I wish I knew if God would hear me if I said a prayer, if—if I told Him I was sorry! because I am, you know, very sorry I've been so wicked. . . . I dare not die like I am. And people do die any day, don't they? One can never tell. I've never been a good girl, or cared about religion; but I'm often so afraid now, Ernest, not when you're with me, but when you're away."

He had laid her back on her pillow, and
was sitting on the bed by her; his elbow
resting upon it, and his head on his hand.
The moonlight shone full and clear upon
them both : his face was in shadow, but
hers was shown plainly; pale, and stained
with tears, and her quantity of fair hair lay
tossed about the pillow. She looked at
Glanville very gravely, and with an expression in the eyes that made his heart beat
like a hammer within his breast. She was
not going to die, surely ?

" I don't know what to say to you, Nora.
I am afraid I don't pray."

" I know you don't; but arn't you ever
afraid like me ? Don't you ever think of
death, or anything horrible like that ?"

" Not much. If I do, I drive the thoughts
away at once. That's what you should
do. It does no good to think of dreadful
things."

" But, Ernest, it's got to come some day !
I thought I was dying once when I was ill,
and I was terrified. I shall never forget it.
.   .   .   But do you think I really am quite

well now ?   Did the doctor say I was ?" she
asked after a little pause.

" Of course he did.   He said you wanted
nothing but change of air and scene.   And
this air has done you an immense deal of
good.   But you mustn't get into the blues,
you know, and mope and go on as you have
been doing just now.   There—there's your
fleur d'oranger, drink it off."

" What are you all doing downstairs ?"
she asked.   " You seem so happy and
cheerful !"

" I shouldn't have been happy and cheerful if I'd known you were making yourself
miserable all this time.   I am going to bring
you up something to eat and drink, and a
light.   I shall send to Lyons for the carriage
to-morrow, and we'll be off again.   I would
never have stayed so long here, but that the
air seemed to suit you so well.   Now, are
you all right again ?"

She told him she was.   What else could
she tell him ?   And he went downstairs.

" I wonder," thought Ernest, as he stood
in the kitchen, while the kind-hearted and

clever little landlady bustled about to pre-
pare a tray for " Madame," and her son
went into the cellar to bring up a bottle of
especial wine for her. " I wonder if I could
work the convent idea after all. It looks
to me as if there were a good opening.
Poor child—how strange, and pale, and un-
like herself she looked !" and he shuddered,
as if the room were cold, and turned towards
the fire.

*   *   *   *   *

Ernest began, after this, to take great apparent interest in external and internal
church architecture. He would stop the
carriage at almost every church they passed,
and the churches, even in these remote
villages, were often gorgeously and taste-
fully decorated ; rich in silver and lace ; in
pictures, altars, and flowers. There were
always exquisite offerings of violets, lilies,
and roses before the Virgin's shrine ; and
screened from the heat and glare of day,
the worshippers, chiefly women, knelt, in
their dark dresses and pure white caps, with
faces ever turned towards the soft radiance

of the altar ; eyes, serenely and steadfastly fixed on the Holy Mother's face, which remained for ever bent upon that of her Child.

Nora—either from listlessness, or because the cool and quiet were grateful to her, or impelled by a nameless sentiment which was growing day by day stronger in her, and making her graver and sadder, would often sit for half an hour at a time, gazing in silence on a Virgin's face, or on the flowers and little glimmering tapers at her feet. Sometimes she talked to Ernest of what she felt ; and now, instead of discouraging such conversation, he affected so much sympathy with, and perception of, her meaning ; he talked so well, and as it seemed, so reasonably, on the subject of Catholic institutions, praising the warmth, the poetry, the beauty of its ordinances, that Nora, looking at him in astonishment one day, said,

" Ernest, are you going to turn Roman Catholic ? or are you one already ? You have often told me you were nothing !"

" Well, I believe I'm going to be a Roman

Catholic one of these days," replied Mr. Glanville. " I've a great liking for Roman Catholic forms. Protestantism is too cold. *Arrêtez!*" he called out to the driver. "What is that building? Is it a convent?"

" Yes, Monsieur. That is the convent of Véguery."

" Stop a moment, and let us look at it. There now, Nora, what becomes of one's English ideas of a convent—alias, a prison —in face of such a one as that? A pretty, roomy, country or farm-house, in a garden, with a *clocher;* a pretty statue of the Virgin in a niche ; the abbess' parlour window open, and the green and white curtains fluttering in the breeze. Nothing but the two ecclesiastical-looking portals there to make it look as if anything were shut in, or shut out !"

Nora leaned her chin on her hand, and looked at the convent in silence for some time. It was just what Ernest wanted, and he smoked on quietly, not saying a word to interrupt her meditations. After a minute or two, a light spring-cart passed them at a

good pace, and was driven up to the gates.
A robust farmer alighted from it, and handed
down two sweet-looking, fair-faced nuns,
who thanked him in very cheerful, pretty
French for the trouble he had taken in
bringing them so far. They wore, of course,
black dresses and veils, with a white
" coiffure " across their brows and down
the sides of their faces; and each carried
a neat silk umbrella, to screen her from the
sun.

" Were not they pretty women ?" asked
Glanville, as the two drove on again. " And
didn't they look as if they led happy and
peaceful lives ?"

(He would have drowned himself, of
course, before attempting any such life on
his own account.)

" Yes," answered Nora, quietly, " very
happy and peaceful ;" and she added, with
a simplicity that half vexed and half amused
him, " They must have quite different
natures to other women."

" Why ?" asked Ernest.

" Because they have chosen of their own

accord to live without any gaiety, or any change, or anything that makes life pleasant."

" Oh !—— is that the view you take of it ?" inquired her lover, beginning to regret the amount of time they had lost in churches.

" Well, they don't have any pleasures, do they ?"

" I suppose they have the pleasure of feeling they are leading good lives," returned Mr. Glanville, with great seriousness.

Nora said no more.

They had come to a village—a large, pretty village, with old Venetian blinds outside the windows, ledges and balconies filled with pots of flowers, doorways draped and crowned with the green and loaded vine : a village where there were tufty little trees in front of shops and cafés ; a fountain, at which the women, in their great straw hats, with red and green jars of ancient shape, were standing in groups and chattering : a village through which passed rude carts, drawn by oxen or mules, with long fringes nearly covering their faces, and with tinkling bells at the side, to herald their approach. Here they descended at a little inn, with a tiny parlour, looking into a garden crammed with rock-work and flowers ; eat fruit and *pain brioche,* and drank coffee, and then went on again.

Went on, hour after hour, day after day, week after week, to be pursued perpetually and pitilessly by the avenging shadow that darkened the loveliest day ; forced itself between them and the sweetest scenes ; weighed upon the heart, when the heart would be buoyant ; forced back every rising of the soul, every natural impulse of gaiety ; poisoned every cup and every morsel, every hour of life and every hour of rest!

The last scene of their French travel was a somewhat memorable one to both. It occurred in this way.

The driver of their little carriage proposed one day, to Mr. Glanville, an excursion to an old château, at some miles distance up the valley. It could be seen throughout, he said, by giving a franc or two to the old concièrge, and was worth seeing. Thither accordingly they went.

The château was situated deep down in a hollow among its own green woods. It had stood for about two hundred years, and was a plain white, oblong mass of building, with three regular rows of windows, a court-yard in front, and a great iron gate, guarded by a ferocious dog, who was chained up before the visitors were allowed to enter. The concièrge, who could hardly walk for age and rheumatism, took one or two rusty keys from a nail in the wall of his little lodge, and preceded them to the house. The old kitchen, which he first showed them, was vaulted, like the crypts of a church, and there were pieces of furniture and various cooking utensils of a great age, all thrown about the floor in disorder. The wide old chimney looked black and cold; the cupboards were empty, and full of dirt and dust, nothing was cared for or cleaned. The dining-room was very large, but looked desolate enough, with its four undraped windows, and its rough brick floor. There were some pictures, a mirror and a bureau left in it. In the drawing-room on the same floor, there was a multitude of old prints, framed in black, and apparently dating from the time of Louis XV. or XVI., and which were ranged regularly, and close together, round the walls ; there were also chairs of old-fashioned shape, covered with faded silk, and lastly a mirror, in an old, but splendidly-carved gilt frame. In the bedrooms of this desolate and deserted place, there still stood great four-posted beds, hung with what had once been splendid silk damasks ; blue, rose, amber, or lavender— or else with red cloth, much moth-eaten ; but all had hearse-like plumes, of the same colour as the hangings. In these rooms there were also mirrors, in exquisitely carved and gilt frames, old furniture, portraits (in oil), of ladies in ruffs and powdered hair, and long, stiff, jewelled corsets ; and one, of a little girl—almost a baby—all stiffly dressed and coiffed. Everything was more or less falling to ruin, but everything was alike neglected.

Last of all, the old man showed his visitors into a smaller room than the others, and one in which there were a few very common articles of modern furniture. In some of the grander bed-rooms there were handsome tapestries, and chairs, worked in fine worsted and silks ; here there was a common paper, and a few old cane-bottomed chairs. The mattresses were thrown up untidily on the bed, and on the hearth were the ashes of a fire, lighted there three years ago.

"What room was this ?" Ernest asked ; "did anyone sleep there now ?" He thought the ashes were only a few days, or at most a few weeks old.

"It was the master's room, when he was a boy," returned the old concièrge ; "so when he was last here he chose to sleep in it. No one has ever been in it since."

"And how long was that ago ?" asked Glanville.

"That was three years ago," replied the old man, with his dull grey eyes fixed vacantly upon the dusty and ash-covered hearth before him. "Yes, that was more than three years ago. Monsieur lives in Paris. He never comes here."

"But in England," put in Nora—she spoke with a little faltering in her voice—"we are so proud of our country houses! we keep them always in repair, and live in them. We never let them go to ruin like this!"

"Ah, indeed, madame?" responded the concièrge, with a sudden accent of sharpness in his voice, and betraying more animation than he had hitherto shown, "but suppose you, in England, learnt to detest a place, so that you didn't care to live in it; what then?"

Nora looked at the man, and so did Glanville, but they neither of them spoke.

"Suppose you would rather see it go to ruin, than have anything more to do with it, eh? How would you English feel then?"

He was a sour and cross old man, and was evidently somewhat incensed at the lady's having drawn any comparison between the two nations. His eyes had an angry gleam in them as he looked at her.

"Well, tell us the story," said Ernest; "and then we shall understand you. Madame had no intention of offending you."

The story is very simple," replied the old man ; "and not new, monsieur. Three years ago, as I told you, the master came down here from Paris. He came to have some rooms put in readiness for the ' accouchement' of his wife. She had taken a fancy, she said, that she should recover better in the air of the country than in Paris, and she wished her son to be born in the old château of his ancêtres. She was monsieur's cousin, but much younger than he was ; they had been brought up in this old château together. She was confined here, and the child died."

" And she . . . ?" continued Nora, who had listened in almost breathless attention up to this point in the man's story.

" And she," said the old man, turning on her his dull, cold eyes, "and she ran away from this house with her doctor— who had been an old flame of hers ; and whom she would have married before, if she had had her way. She left from this house in broad day, going out of one of the garden gates as if she were only going to the village ; and she was never seen any more."

As he finished speaking, the man turned round, and with apparent indifference, and almost apathy of manner and expression, hobbled out of the room, dangling his rusty keys in his hand. As they passed an open window in one of the corridors, he looked out of it, and swore at his dog, who was barking and howling frightfully in the courtyard below ; then stumped slowly down the stairs, followed by the man and woman who had just been listening to his story.

" The master fell just here," said the concièrge, indicating a spot on the pavement, at the bottom of the great stair-case. " He left his regiment, and came to see his wife for a few days—thinking to take her back to Paris with him—he knew nothing ;—and they told him just here— where I stand. He fell right back, as if he were shot ; and Jacques and I picked him up. He's never been here since."

*   *   *   *

CHAPTER X.

THE winter and early spring were spent in Naples : in April, the heat became too great for Nora's strength, and they set off northwards by easy stages ; intending when they reached France, to stay a short time at X—— ; then go on to Strasburg, and from Strasburg to Germany.

For some time past, Glanville had taken to a certain amount of amateur gaming, as a " distraction ;" and it distracted him a good deal. Before they had left France at the beginning of the winter, he had yielded to the charm of French gaming-tables—as well as to other charms—and since then, his evenings had been spent constantly away from the unfortunate woman who depended

upon him, for her one and only distraction. He was not mad enough, or hot-
headed enough to play high ; but he amused
himself with play, sometimes excited himself with it ; and at the least and worst,
contrived by means of it to get through so
many hours in the week. At such times he
fancied he was almost inured to the life he
was forced to lead ; but much oftener he
rebelled against it with miserable restless-
ness, and sought how he might end it " and
begin afresh."

They had reached France, and were staying for a short time in one of the quietest
hotels in X—— (Lady Glanville, be it
said here, contrived to keep her favourite
son supplied with money, much as she had
disapproved, and still disapproved, of his
conduct), when one afternoon, an English
letter was brought up to them, addressed
to " M. Osborne," the name which Glanville
had assumed since he left England. The
letter—or rather note—was from his mother,
and ran as follows :—

" MY DEAR ERNEST,

"Your brother Sidney is very ill, and scarcely expected to recover. If you wish to see him, you must come at once. Your father will not allow me to write more, and it is only for Sidney's sake, that he has allowed me to write this.

" Your affectionate mother,
" HARRIET GLANVILLE."

Ernest started up from his lounging-chair and his *Galignani*, and threw the letter across the table to Nora. He waited for a moment while she read it, in blank and pale dismay; and then said, "You see I haven't a moment to lose. I must go at once."

" Go at once, Ernest—and leave me ?"

" My dearest—it is only for a week or two. What can I do ? You would not wish to come with me ?"

" I cannot—so there is no use thinking what I wish. Oh, Ernest," the poor girl went on, clasping him with her arms, and trembling with terror, " promise not to

stay!   Promise   me   to'   come back, will
you ?"

Glanville hesitated for a moment.   Here,
at last, was the opportunity for which he
had longed; an opening in the stifling
hedge of his imprisonment through which
he saw light—through which he felt air.
Mingled feelings of relief, at the idea of
escape and freedom—of anxiety and sorrow
respecting his brother—of fear of leaving
Nora—of dread of her future if he did—
and yet an over-mastering sense of resolve,
even in that moment, that he would leave
her ; and if possible, leave her for ever,—
threw such sudden tumult into his heart,
as it had never felt before.   He had behaved, for the most part, with what poor
honour, consideration and tenderness towards her he could ; that is, when he was
with her he had tried to atone, in his way,
for the great wrong he had done her ; but
he had felt for a long time that his
patience and his endurance were at an end.
He had come to understand the feeling
which makes a man act the part of a brute,

after he has acted that of a villain; makes him desert the woman he has ruined, because he can endure his regrets, his disillusion, and his state of "quarantine" no longer. Still — he could not tell her in words, and now, that she would see him no more. He must deceive her still a little longer.

"What are you thinking of, Nora? Of course I shall come back to you," said her lover.

"Are you sure?" she asked, detecting, with the quickness of fear, something a little unusual and unsatisfactory in his voice and manner.

"Of course, I am sure," he answered, impatiently; "why do you worry me so, when you see I must be off at once? Where did you put the key of my portmanteau?"

But instead of answering him, Nora threw herself on her sofa, and burst into tears. He had never spoken in that tone to her before.

"Tell me where my key is, for God's

sake," continued Ernest, in a fume; "you said you had it. Do you want my brother to die before I see him ?"

She took the keys from her pocket, and threw them on to the floor without a word.

Glanville took them up and slammed himself out of the room. He had never been really impatient with her till now, and now he was cruel : cruel in the first moment that his thoughts of leaving her took definite and positive form. When he had half packed his portmanteau, however, he came back, and went on his knees beside her.

" I was a great brute to you, just now, Nora. I shall never forgive myself if I have hurt you. But I am worried and harassed, and it's such short notice for everything. I ought to be off by the next train, you see. There—kiss me, and forgive me, my own dear, poor girl !"

An hour afterwards the carriage was at the door, which must take him away.

She drove with him to the station ; and when it was reached, Ernest got out, and standing by the door of the carriage, took both her hands in his. She held them with her own, tightly clasped in her lap, and looked into his face. Her eyes were red with crying, and her face very pale ; but she spoke with almost unnatural calm.

" You will write to me, Ernest ?" she said.

" The moment I am in England, my darling."

" Not before ?"

" Well, from Paris, if you like."

" You will not forget—" her voice broke here ; but recovering herself with a steady self-possession that surprised him, she went on, " You will not forget how utterly lonely I shall be without you ?" The words struck like a stab to his heart. For a moment he could not speak.

" I shall not forget it," he answered in an unsteady voice. " I shall always think of you."

" Well, then—good-bye."

He had meant that they should part thus. He felt that anything else would have been intolerable. Perhaps she felt it too.

He waited to see her driven off, and to

wave his hand to her, as she kissed hers, before losing sight of him.

When she reached home she locked herself into her room, and flung herself on her bed, in an agony of grief.

"I shall never see him again! I saw it in his face. He has left me—left me for ever! Oh, God! have mercy on me! What am I to do?"

*   *   *   *   *

Sidney's life hung on a thread for many days. At last, however, he was pronounced out of danger, and in process of time, regained almost his usual amount of health and strength. When he was sufficiently recovered to travel, he was ordered change; and Ernest went with him into Scotland, where they stayed a long time, the family remaining until late in the autumn in —— shire. Ernest kept his promise of writing to Nora, and he wrote often, and kindly. She answered him, and answered him at length, because she had nothing else to do; but the settled conviction, amounting to a presentiment in her mind that Ernest would not return to her, was scarcely ever really shaken for a day.

In her unprotected position she could scarcely either walk or drive out in X—— without exciting attention, and attention of a kind she dreaded. To give any description, therefore, of the weariness, the suspense, the depression by day, and the misery by night, the utter desolation of heart and spirit endured, during six awful weeks, by this deserted woman, were a task so unspeakably painful, that heart and pen alike fail before it, and refuse to take it up.

The wife of the hotel " propriétaire" had a little child, about three years old, and this child Nora would have in her room by the hour together, nursing it, hearing its imperfect chatter, and sometimes even letting it sleep upon her bed. She began, in sheer despair at her enforced idleness, to work for it; she made it pretty pinafores; tied ribbon into sashes for it, and would coax it with bon-bons to let her curl its hair. She was not naturally fond of children, and this " petite fille" was probably the first child she had ever cared for. As it was, its innocent companionship, and the cheerful, kind-hearted, sympathising talk of the good " bonne" who would bring the little thing to her room, and fetch it away again ; added to a certain amount of amusement to be got out of the " femme de chambre" who attended to her rooms, and who seemed to be a sort of grown-up " Topsy" in manners, customs, and almost in complexion; lastly, the civility, kindliness, and compassion of the good "dame de l'hôtel" herself, probably prevented Nora from sinking into a fever, from mere loneliness, misery, and anxiety.

The heat in X—— had become almost unendurable, but the poor girl was too hopeless and wretched to care to move, even had she known where to go to. Deep down somewhere, in a far corner of her heart, there must have lurked at times a faint, faint hope that her lover would return to her ; for when his letters came, she tore them eagerly open, glanced through them before reading them, turned

the sheet this way and that, to make
sure she had not missed a line or word,
and then, leaning back on her couch,
would press both hands over her eyes,
and shed hot and bitter tears.

When he had been away about a month,
Mr. Glanville wrote a letter, which, though
it said nothing at all about his coming back,
roused Nora in rather a peculiar manner,
and made her feel as if exertion on her part
were not only becoming advisable, but
would soon become necessary. We have
said before, that when touched on a certain
point, she could show—as, we suppose,
every living woman who is not an idiot (let
her be frivolous, or let her be wise) can show
—a certain amount of both pride and dignity. The time had come at last—and it
came rather suddenly—for showing both.

Mr. Glanville entreated her, in point of
fact, to throw herself, head and neck—body
and soul, rather—into the bosom of the
Roman Catholic Church. He was afraid
she would think it was a very serious letter
he was going to write ; but he had had the

subject in his mind a long time, and was determined at last to put it before her in the strongest light he could. He had felt, himself, for years, though he had never talked much on the subject (this last assertion was undeniably true), that if there was a religion which was to do any good in the world it was the religion he spoke of. He could not, of course, say much to guide her as to details, or as to her best way of beginning; but he was sure Madame Bochet would be able to give her all the information she required. He supposed she would only have to seek out a priest—perhaps to confess herself to him—be introduced to the superior of a convent, and the whole thing would be managed as quickly and easily as possible. Any priest would seize on the opportunity of such a conversion. There would be no earthly difficulty ; and was it not—was it not, after all—almost the only course left open to her ? If she reflected seriously for only five minutes, he thought she would see it was. If she had any insuperable objection to the Roman Catholic Church—

though he had fancied, while they were travelling together, that he saw signs of the contrary feeling—would she have the same objection to joining one of the Protestant Sisterhoods of Germany? He remembered to have heard them spoken of by his sisters' German governess, who had a relation " in one of them ;" and he believed she represented the life as being a very useful and happy, and not at all a confined, one. He had no doubt she could gain any information she wanted from the Protestant pastor in X——. He would be able to give her the addresses of German pastors, or tell her where she could obtain them. She might think it unfeeling in him to write in this way ; but he firmly believed the day would come when she would thank him for doing so. There was, after all, another world and another life after this. He was afraid they had both forgotten this too much. He knew he was the last person on earth to dare to write to her of these things, and it covered him with remorse to feel it was so ; but might he not, even at this eleventh hour,

try to make a little reparation for the wrong
he had done her, by urging on her a step
which he was perfectly convinced would be
for her temporal and her spiritual welfare ?

" And now, my dear Nora," he con-
cluded, " don't imagine that, while I am
using every argument to show you the
advantage—if not the positive necessity—
of taking up some such life as this, I am
planning for myself a return to all the
pleasures and distractions I used to enjoy.
I feel only too well and too bitterly that
I have lost my place in society for many
years, perhaps for ever. I have no idea
of remaining in England. I shall get a
commission in the Indian Army, and go
out. I dare say you may think you are
the worst off, but you have little idea
how filled with gloom and depression I
am at times. And the mention of India
brings me to a part of my letter which
it is very painful to me to write, and which
I am afraid it will be painful to you to read.
I dare say you have noticed that I have
said nothing hitherto about returning to

you. I observe, too, that you say very little to me (in direct words, at least,) on that most painful of subjects. I have fancied, sometimes, that there has been throughout —in spite of my rash promise to you when I left X——,—a sort of tacit understanding between us that we had better meet no more. I will not, my dear Nora, say a word to pain you, or to remind you of the unhappy past. I will only say that everything was becoming worse ; our fault, in fact, was becoming greater every day that we remained together. I am quite certain you will feel with me in this ; in fact, you cannot do otherwise. I was often very wretched in thinking what I had brought you to.

" Then, my dear Nora, there is another thing ; though, as you have a great dislike to talk about business and money matters, I will only say a few words about it. I am afraid I cannot go on, without great inconvenience, sending you the money which is necessary for your expenses. We both know how things mount up, and I am

already in debt on every hand ; and my
father, as you know, has grudged giving
me the money he has been forced to do. I
say ' forced,' because he is not yet in the
least reconciled with me ; in fact, we cannot
live in the same house together. He has
told Sidney he will pay off my debts and
continue a certain allowance to me, if I
accept a commission abroad ; and you know,
I dare say, how awfully expensive living is
in India. Canada I don't care for. To
conclude, I feel quite convinced that you
have sufficient regard for me not to wish
all my prospects in life to be blasted,
which they would be, my dear girl, if
we continued to live together. You are
aware, of course, how very uncertain poor
Sidney's life is, and that he will never
marry ; and, of course, after my father's
death I shall be head of the family.
This being the case, I ought to marry ;
and I think it better for us both that I
should tell you so plainly, and then you
will see what a difficult position I am in.
I would write more, but I fear my letter

will only just catch the post as it is, and I don't want to delay sending it. Let me hear from you at once. I shall be very anxious and unsettled until I do so. And now, my dear Nora,

"I remain, always,

"Yours, very sincerely and faithfully,

"ERNEST GLANVILLE."

It was not a bad letter; and it was, on the whole, a remarkably faithful transcript of Ernest's feelings at the time he wrote. He had spent more time and thought over it than he had ever bestowed on a composition in his life. When it was finished, and he had read it over, he took it in his hand, and seating himself at the head of Sidney's sofa, so that the latter could not see his face, threw it over in front of him.

"Do you mind reading that, Sidney, before it goes?"

"What is it?"

"Well, you'll see directly. Read from here to there," said Ernest, pointing with his finger to the places where Sidney was to begin and to finish.

Mr. Glanville began, and read slowly and in silence, till he came to the words, " Canada I don't care about," where he was to stop.   Then he put the letter down.

" Well ?" inquired Ernest.

" What are you prepared to do, if she does not accept either of your propositions?" asked Mr. Glanville, looking up towards him.

" To do ?" repeated Ernest.

" Yes ; what is to become of her, if she doesn't choose to be a nun ?" said Sidney.

" Confound me—I don't know. I haven't thought of it," returned Ernest, after an uneasy silence of several minutes.

" Well, but you will have to think of it, won't you ?"

" It's all nonsense, Sidney.   She *must* do something of the sort.   There's no help for it."

" Look here, Ernest.   No matter what you sacrifice, you mustn't leave her in France, of all earthly places, without money, and without protection.   If she won't do as you wish her, you must provide for her in some way, whatever you deny your-self."

"And why on earth must I provide for her in some way?" inquired Ernest, rapidly, and a little hotly. "I don't see what business it is of mine any longer." He got up and stood leaning against the mantelpiece, with his hands in his pockets, and his hand-some face considerably flushed.

"I can't talk to you off there," said his brother ; " come where I can see you. What do you mean by saying it is no business of yours any longer ?"

"Because I don't believe it is."

"Then I disagree with you entirely. I don't say *what* you ought to do, but you can't throw off all responsibility in this easy way."

"How can you expect to know anything of these things?" retorted Ernest ; "you who lie on a sofa from one year's end to another? It's absurd to tell me I am re-sponsible. You know as well as I do, though no one else knows it, that she made me take her away. I held out against it

till she lay half dead in my arms, after saying she would go out and drown herself.
It is not my fault that we have lived together—and now you know what I think."

He walked up to the window, and stood
for some time looking out of it, then turned,
and paced the room several times from end
to end.

" It was your fault that she ever wanted
your protection for a day or for an hour,"
replied Sidney, briefly. " I suppose you
have not forgotten that ?"

" We've been over that folly, Sidney, again
and again," returned his brother, with
irritation ; " and you know everything, and
you oughtn't to think of me so hardly. Don't
let us talk of it ; it gives me the horrors."
After a little pause, he went on, " I believe
you are to be envied after all, that you can
lie here year after year, without knowing
anything of the temptations and miseries a
fellow meets with in the world."

"Do you suppose, then, I know nothing of
them," inquired Sidney.

" You cannot.   It is simply and practically impossible. In the first place, do you know what love or passion, call it what you like, is, Sidney? Have you ever been in love in your life ?"

Now, we regret not to be able to state that Mr. Glanville, upon having this query propounded to him, either "flushed up suddenly, and in a painful manner ;" and after a few moments' silence, said in a changed and husky voice, " Don't ask me, for God's sake. Talk of something else !" or that he became "suddenly of an ashy paleness ; his face showing agitated workings, which it was impossible to repress," &c., &c. It is, on the contrary, our bounden duty to assert, that Sidney only answered with remarkable coolness—

" We will keep to your own affairs, if you please. If I have ever been in love it has been in a way very innocuous to other people, if not to myself ; a thing which can't be said of your love affairs, or rather entanglements. Ernest, I want to know what you are going to do about——what you are going to do in case this conventual scheme comes to nothing ?"

" I shall tell her she had better write to her husband, do the repentant, and see what comes of it," replied his brother, with a sort of reckless hardihood in his tone ; " that's what I shall do."

" Oh, well, if you will do that," said Sidney, rather suddenly, taking up his newspaper, " I have no more advice to give. I don't say you will be wrong, I don't say you will be right ; perhaps you will be right. It is a peculiar step, that's all." There was a long silence, broken by Ernest saying at last,

" Sidney, where is Arthur ?"

" I don't know."

" You don't know ?"

" No ; but I might be able to tell you in a week or two."

" Does he write to you ?"

" He writes a few lines, or sends his card with an address on it, now and then."

" What for ?"

" That I may tell him if at any time I

know of his wife being in any want or distress." After which remark, both the brothers observed a complete silence for several minutes.

" And of course I shall do it," pursued Sidney, with an expression on his mouth, and in his eyes, which Ernest had not often seen there before, "if you oblige me to do it."

" You will do nothing of the sort," exclaimed Ernest. " What do you take me for ? I would go without a coat to my back before you should do it. *You* write to him indeed ! . . . It would be a different thing if she did."

" Has she got money now, Ernest, or has she not ?" asked his brother. " Are you leaving her in such a position that she *must* take refuge in a convent, or write to her husband, one or the other ? I only want to know that. I swore to Longley that I would not let her be in distress, to my knowledge, without telling him."

" She is not in distress."

" You are certain of that ?"

" "I sent her some money a few days ago. Do you think I would lie to you, Sidney? I'm not such a brute as to want her to starve, if you think I am. But I want to end matters now," continued Ernest, with a sort of dogged resolution in his tone; " and I shall try my best to end them. It is the only course left to me. And a convent life is the best thing she can take to. Don't you believe she will go into a convent?" he added, as he looked fixedly at his brother.

"I should judge not, from what I've seen of her—and heard of her." Ernest reflected for a few minutes.

"Hang Protestantism!" he exclaimed at last, with sudden and rather violent emphasis; "it doesn't leave the women a loop-hole anywhere. What was she brought up a Protestant for? What good has it done her? It hasn't prevented ——" he stopped short. "Never mind," he continued; "it's done now, and I've said the right thing in the letter. There's no doubt about that, no matter what she does." And then Ernest directed and stamped his letter, and threw it into his desk, ready for posting the next morning.

The last thing he said was, " I can't think how Arthur came to make such a miss, as not to settle any money on her when he was married. If he had done, she would have been independent; and it would have saved all this worry !"

CHAPTER XI.

WHEN Nora received Mr. Glanville's epistle, she read it through dry-eyed; and with her heart beating an indignant and resistant throb, to almost every word !

She was not entirely without principle ; and not more devoid of a certain religious feeling—or perhaps we should say, fear— than are many women, brought up in the way, and by the sort of mother that she had been. She did not therefore believe that Ernest was wrong, in saying that " their fault became greater every day that they remained together ;" and she did not at all times really wish that he should re- turn to her : but her pride and her heart alike rebelled at her betrayer being the man to bring before her the sense of her shame, and the " necessity " for a change of life. The last part of the letter, which Ernest had purposely made short " because she disliked talk about business and money matters," roused all the blood she had in her.

" There were once a hundred reasons for not ringing some church-bells, for some king or other," said Nora, flinging Ernest's letter on to the table, with a flushed face and angry beams in her eyes ; " and the hundredth was, that there were no bells ! There are ninety-nine excellent reasons for my becoming a nun ; but the hundredth is, that Mr. Glanville will send me no more money."

She had never been excited into making such a speech as that, in her life before.

An hour afterwards, she was in tears, and sobbing upon the sofa ; and had to tell Françoise, when she brought " *la petite Julie,*" that she had heard very bad news from her husband; and had the " migraine " in consequence, and Julie must go away.

The next day she advertised herself in
the principal X——journal, as an English
lady " who would be glad to give lessons in
her own language." The advertisement
passed unheeded ; and a few days afterwards, she advertised in two "*journaux;*"
and by Mme. Bochet's advice, had some
cards printed, which the good-natured lady
undertook to distribute among the various
" magasins " where she dealt. These
efforts also producing no result, Nora,
after spending a week in a miserable state
of annoyance, disappointment, and per-
plexity, determined to advertise for a third
and last time ; altering the advertisement
to, " An English lady desires a situation
immediately as English, or English and
musical teacher, in a school or family." It
was evident that a " religious life " in a
Roman Catholic convent, had not yet become the poor girl's highest earthly ideal !

Two days after this third attempt at
advertising, Jules, the waiter, showed into
Mme. Osborne's room, a gentleman, upon
whose card was written in large, black
German characters—

"M. Carl August Höffner."

Nora had been left a humbled, and a somewhat intimidated woman by her time of desertion and of sorrow; she did not look now, as she sat at work in that plain little room, as if she had been the "fashion" of two London seasons. She rose very hurriedly, as M. Höffner was announced; her heart beating fast, and her face turning paler than usual. After the two had bowed to each other, and she had requested the gentleman to seat himself, M. Höffner proceeded to explain that he had only the day before seen "Madame's" advertisement in the newspaper. He had just returned from a business journey to Paris. He was in want of an English teacher for his four eldest children; some one who would come to his house every morning in the week, and remain till after breakfast; and on two days remain till three o'clock, to give lessons to his two eldest boys who attended the "Lycée." The children had had a resident English governess for a year, but she had left three months ago; and the young ones

were forgetting all their English. An
omnibus left from a " place " very near this
hotel, and passed the very door of M.
Höffner's country house, which was rather
more than a mile out of X——. He should
beg Madame to come early in the morning,
to avoid the greatest heat ; say about eight
o'clock ; but in this she could of course
please herself. "At St. Pierre," he said,
" they all went to bed about half-past eight
or nine, and rose at six or earlier." He
had taken the liberty of demanding " *des
renseignements* " regarding Madame, " *en
bas.*" He was quite satisfied ; he heard that
her husband had been obliged to return to
England on pressing and unfortunate business, and that she wished to occupy herself
a little in the meantime. It was, of course,
just a chance that he required an English
teacher ; just a chance that he had seen her
advertisement ; but having done so, and
having half an hour to spare from his
business, he had just come to ascertain
whether, etc., etc., etc.

Nora reflected. It would be harder work

than she had ever known in her life, and harder also than she had strength for. But she longed with a feverish longing to be able to write and tell Ernest, that she would no longer be a burden to him. This was a beginning; she might get other pupils; Mme. Bochet had said she would get "*un maître de piano*," of her acquaintance, to recommend her to schools, and in the families where he taught. Well, yes :—she would accept.

As M. Höffner sat before her, on a low chair, not a very handsome one—("Madame Osborne" had changed her quarters to a very small room "au troisième" since she began advertising), holding his new and perfectly brushed hat in his hands, she had ample opportunities for taking in the points of his appearance. He was a florid complexioned Frankforter, with rugged features, which she could easily imagine stern;—grey, bushy eyebrows ; rather light-brown hair, streaked with grey, but very glossy, and carefully arranged ; small, quick, irascible blue eyes ; a thick moustache, and a stout, commanding figure.

When it had been arranged that Mme.
Osborne should commence giving her lessons on the following morning, and terms
had been discussed (they were not very
remunerative terms to "Madame," or very
ruinous ones to "Monsieur"), the latter
took his departure.

* * * * *

"Eh bien—as-tu vu ta dame anglaise?"
inquired Höffner's French partner, when
that gentleman had re-entered his ware-
house, and was seated at his desk.

"Oui, je l'ai vue," replied Höffner, briefly,
as he lighted his cigar, preparatory to re-
suming work.

"Et qu'en penses-tu? Est-elle bien?"

"Je n'en sais rien," answered the German.

"However, you have engaged her?"

"Yes; I have engaged her."

"You are singular, Höffner!" said his
friend.

"They told me at the hotel (where she
has been for some time it appears,) that she
was a married woman. Elle en avait l'air,
c'est tout ce que je sais! Her husband

has made 'des mauvaises affaires,' and has gone to England to retrieve himself, if he can, and doesn't wish his wife to come to him till he can provide her with a home.— Is it true? What do I know? Probably it's not—the half of it."

And M. Höffner commenced turning over his papers, while he blew a succession of short puffs from his cigar.

"I thought you were almost afraid of your daughter speaking to any woman but her own mother," remarked his friend and partner, "and now you send, God knows who, to teach her English, and what else she likes, every morning of the week!"

"She is 'lady-like;' she has a good accent" (Höffner, be it observed, spoke French fluently, but like the German born, bred, and educated that he was), "c'est tout ce qu'il me faut. Du reste, que ma femme s'en charge. Il me faut une per-sonne anglaise pour mes enfants; et voilà tout. I had fine references with the other," he continued, "and we agreed together, n'est-ce pas?"

M. Brunet laughed, and went on with his work.

"Diable !" recommenced the other, after a short pause, "I take every one into my house, and send every one out of it, for my own convenience, not theirs. Young ladies have precious few opportunities of playing the coquette at St. Pierre, je te promets."

"Take care your English lady, whose husband is in England, or 'en Espagne,'" said M. Brunet, "doesn't find out how to play it, and teach Louise. Louise is very young ; at her age one must be careful."

"Louise will tell her mother or me everything 'cette Anglaise' does or says during the whole time she is with us," replied Höffner, "and at the end of a month we shall have her measure perfectly. Then we put her out of the door, or keep her, as we choose; voilà tout. If she is 'convenable,' I shall make her the offer to stay in the house, and help madame with the children, and her work."   *   *   *

The next morning Nora went up to St. Pierre, to give her first lessons. She rang at a narrow wooden entrance-door, on the left side of a pair of large gates, closed and locked, and on each side of which a high garden wall ran for a considerable distance along the road. In the smaller door was a "guichet," or square opening, to which there was a slide, with bolt attached, and through which, when she had pushed it back, the "bonne," who had been summoned by her ring, looked hurriedly, to ascertain that the visitor was neither a "réligieuse" nor a man—two species of the human kind held (as Nora afterwards found) in a sort of sacred horror at St. Pierre. This point being settled satisfactorily, the door was opened, and the English governess admitted. Her work was then begun.

Nora taught at St. Pierre every morning, and for the two specified afternoons in every week, till a month was over.

During the greater part of this time, Louise, the eldest girl, though not very studious, was "très gentile ;" Master Fritz, though passionate, was tolerably amenable; and the two elder boys, though inclined to be "moqueurs" and "rebelles," managed to keep their inclinations within decent bounds in their worst humours; and the eldest, "August" — a very sweet-looking, dark-eyed fellow of twelve years—when in a good humour, could be wonderfully urbane, docile, and "raisonnable."

Madame Höffner was a German, as well as her husband; and three of the children —Karl, Fritz, and little Hilda—exhibited more of the German than the French elements in their composition; while Louise and August, by way of a pleasing change, presented considerably more of the French than the German type of character. Madame, herself, was a tall, thin lady, with a sweet but rather timid face, brown eyes, and a pleasant, gentle voice. She spoke English and French almost perfectly, but with the German accent (only far less *prononce*) of her husband.

One day it happened that in the midst of her English lesson "Madame Anna," as she was called (Nora had two Christian names, and had been careful only to give the first, and the one which would the least distinguish her), suddenly felt herself oppressed, then became almost breathless, and finally fainted away. Madame and a servant were summoned by the united shrieks of Louise and of Fritz ; and by dint of fanning, of eau-de-cologne, and of the universal panacea, " eau de fleur d'oranger," she was finally revived. It was the heat, she said, which had overcome her. She was not accustomed to the climate of X——, it tried her ; and Fritz, too, had been " fatiguant " that morning. Madame was very tender and pitying. She told the governess not to come the next day, and she kept her till the cool of the evening—in fact, made her dine with them.

The following day Nora received a note, offering her the position of resident English governess in M. Höffner's family, with a salary of twenty-two pounds, "everything found." She was to teach Fritz his general lessons, and to assist madame a little in needle-work. It was time some such offer should come.

The poor girl, with only one pupil besides the Höffners (the son of a "librarien," who paid a franc and a half three times a week, for nearly an hour and a half's lesson each time), had been half starving herself, to avoid asking Glanville for more money. The latter, somewhat pricked in his conscience, had written a letter, begging her not to keep him ignorant of her real circumstances, and to send for what money she required. Appended to this letter, however, was the suggestion that she should appeal to her husband. To tell the truth, Glanville had a horrible fear lest anything worse should befall her than the worst that had happened yet. "Swear to me," he had written in one of his earlier letters, "that nothing shall induce you to form any fresh *liaison.* But I don't believe you will do it, for your husband's sake. In God's name, save him that misery, and me such an insufferable disgrace !" She had sworn ; and had kept her vow, through chances of breaking it, such as are inseparable from the position of an unprotected, a young, and a beautiful woman, alone in an hotel, in the heart of a strange town.

When, however, Mr. Glanville tried his " dernier ressort," in the shape of that suggestion relative to her husband, Nora's' answer to it was that of tearing the sheet into strips, and burning the strips to cinders.

She had long ago repented, with bitter repentance, of her sin ; she had remembered with sickness of heart, and longing that it could be hers again, her husband's unchanging fidelity of affection and care ; but she would not, now that she was deserted by the man for whom she had deserted him, appeal to him for forgiveness and protection. Her last remembrance, besides, of her husband, was of a look of horror and rage, which she could never forget to her dying day ; and since that moment she had never seen or heard of him. She was not only unwilling to appeal to him ; she was afraid of doing so. Had she understood his character, she would have travelled to the ends of the earth to find him, and have thrown herself not at his feet, but on his breast ;

but Nora had never understood her husband, and she believed he must hate her
still.

When, therefore, the situation of resident
English teacher at St. Pierre was offered
her, she felt as if almost an " Arcadia " of
freedom from anxiety and care were opened
to her view.   She wrote at once, accepting
it, and sent a note to Mr. Glanville at the
same time, informing him that "she was
now provided for."   She wrote also to her
sister Lizzie, for the first time since leaving
England.   Then, taking leave of the little
Julie, of Julie's kind mother, and of the
good-hearted Françoise — three human
beings who had been her solace during a
time as miserable and as maddening as a
woman, not actually in want, or physically
suffering, could well pass through : giving
little " cadeaux " to each, and francs she
could ill afford to Jules and to " Topsy "
(in whose black eyes a tear glittered as she
took them), the friendless Englishwoman
seated herself in a shaking omnibus, her
boxes over her head, and rumbled out of

the great town ; finding herself set down,
after half an hour's ride, before the gates of
the Höffner residence.

St. Pierre was a fine specimen of a French
country house, above the average of French
country houses. It was substantially built
of stone, and stood on a stone terrace or
elevation, to which led a short, broad flight
of marble steps, flanked on either side by a
handsome marble vase, filled with training
plants. A verandah was stretched across
the whole front of the house, and brown
Venetian shutters shaded each window.
Forming a wing to the building was a
billiard-room, built in the form of a Swiss
cottage, of stained oak, and with a verandah and balustrade of oak running all round
it ; the whole raised on pillars from below.
The gardens were large and beautiful ; the
ground undulating, so as to form hill, plain,
ravine, and terrace ; there was a large pool,
with a bridge ; an island ; a Chinese summer-
house, and swans ; there were " pavillons,"
(one with striped linen curtains looped to
the round pillars, where the family took

their meals in the early morning or cool evening); there were tables and chairs set out under the trees; there were fruit-trees and flowers in abundance. People visiting St. Pierre, after being cramped all day long in an X—— counting-house, used to say to Höffner, "Mon cher, you possess an earthly Paradise!" With this Paradise we have now somewhat to do.

CHAPTER XII.

LOUISE HÖFFNER, " Madame Anna's " eldest English pupil, was supposed to be receiving a good education ; and a great deal of money was paid to that end. A clever French teacher· came up from X.—— on three mornings in the week, to sit for two hours at a stretch at her elbow, forcing her to hold a pen in her hand, and to read a few pages from a grammar or book of history. This lady (when she was able), or the English governess (when she was not), accompanied Louise once every week to her "cours d'instruction" in town—a very expensive "cours," of which the presiding deity was a tall, intelligent, stylish-looking woman of forty, who had taken "des di-

plomes" in every science of the earth, of
under the earth, and of above the earth.

Mdlle. E—— sat at the end of a long
table, piles of books in front and at the
side of her, and put an infinity of questions
on history, grammar, geography, and science
to the pupils ranged on each side of the
said table ; receiving a correct answer to
about one question in twenty, and giving
the rest herself. The class was held in a
large and handsome room, with mirrors,
statuettes, pictures, polished floor, and
Eastern-looking silk hangings : the pupils
were handsome " nonchalantes " ,French
girls, who knew they would be married in
three, four, or five years, and who had,
therefore, no care in life but to dress themselves, idle away their time in the most
agreeable ways they could invent, and copy
all the airs and graces in others they thought
most bewitching ; of younger and simpler
girls, with less " coquetterie " and more
idea of learning, but for whose capabilities
the " tactics " of the " cours " were far too
extended and advanced (we should rather

say, too unmethodical and desultory) ; of a
few boys, who were looking forward to
being "des Lycéens" in six months, and
who, therefore, thought their present position unworthy of any respect, or of the
expenditure of any effort—(not that they
would honour the "Lycée" with much of
either when they went there) ; and, finally,
of two plain girls—one *bossue*, and the other
of Swiss extraction, who had some intelligence and some idea of application, and
whose answers saved the "cours" of Mdlle.
E—— from being one of the veriest farces
by which trusting parents were ever swin-
dled out of their money.

Louise's own ideas concerning what we
may term the *morale* of learning, were of
a sort that were novel to the mind of her
English governess, and would be, let us
hope, novel to the mind of most "institutrices," whether French, German, or English.
She told Nora one day that Mdlle. Isabelle,
the young English lady who left them the
spring previously, had taken infinite pains
with her English and her music, and had

done all she could to make her talk English
with her; " but," said Louise, " I did not
like anybody or anything that took me
away from mamma; and I never shall.   I
never would stay with her, or walk in the
garden with her, instead of with mamma,
if I could help it.   Papa scolded, and of
course blamed Mdlle. Isabelle—mais cela
ne me faisait rien ! . . .   It was the same
when she taught me music.   I know I improved with her a great deal more than
with Mdlle. Picard, papa said so ; papa and
my cousins praised my playing very much,
after I had only learnt a few weeks with
her ; but she was *too particular*, and I
became tired of taking so much pains ; so
I asked mamma to give me lessons, and
she did."

" But that was very unkind to your
governess," said Nora, " who was doing all
she could for you."

" I know it was very méchante," replied
Louise, with a half smile (a peculiar half
smile, which used to make Nora feel in
looking at it, that her own position at St.

Pierre was of the most insecure) ; " but I could not help myself. She was very good ; she used to .write out all my 'analyses,' when I went to my 'leçons de réligion' before my confirmation."

" Then were you not obliged to write them yourself ?"

Louise shrugged her shoulders. " Yes, madame, I ought to have done, but I found it too *ennuyant*. Once, papa said something at dinner about his hoping that I wrote my ' analyses' myself; so mamma took fright, and told me to do the next one alone, and I tried ; but I was so miserable, and cried so much (till I was quite ill), that mamma said I need not do it again."

" Then did you give up Mademoiselle Isabelle's analyses as yours ?" inquired Nora, who was learning by slow degrees, that these children were trained to take no trouble on themselves, and to devolve everything hard, unpleasant, and disagreeable, upon others.

" It was not my fault," answered Louise, with another shrug, " the lessons were too

difficult for me, and I could not go up to
M. Berger without an 'analyse.' Mademoiselle would sometimes make me write half
a dozen lines myself; then I would say, ' I
will tell you what I mean, if you will write
it.' Then I would study my notes, but
never could make anything out of them, so
she had to read me hers. Then she would
begin, ' Do you remember this ? do you
believe all that ? do you feel the other ?'
and so on. And I used to say, ' Oh, yes,
mademoiselle, perfectly ! it will do to put it
down just as you have it there.' Of course
she couldn't do exactly that; so finally, she
had simply to write all my recollections
herself, and then I copied them out. You
can imagine, madame, it would have been a
little too much to go through all that trouble
with me every time !"

" And did Mademoiselle Isabelle understand and write French well enough to do
all that ?" inquired Nora.

" Je crois bien," answered Louise, laughing ; " she understood French grammar and
composition far better than I do. It was

drôle sometimes to hear M. Berger say
before all the class, and the ladies, you
know, ' Voilà une analyse de Louise Höffner
qui m'a beaucoup plu!' or to see ' A—A'
written before a paragraph, which means
'Très bien, très bien.' But, ah, bah! she
was *Anglaise*, you see, and you English can
work so desperately hard at anything."

It required a person gifted with a faculty
for " desperate work," to pursue in any way,
or by any means, the education, English or
otherwise, of the young Höffners. The
poor governess's worst trials at St. Pierre
were the English lessons and, Fritz's general lessons, which came off (whenever that
young gentleman did not succeed in hiding
himself, or whenever he did not simply and
absolutely refuse to do them), both morning
and afternoon of every day. It was M.
Höffner's wish, that August and Carl should
have an hour's English instruction every
half holiday; and Nora had never known
such a trial in her whole life, as the trial
which these two young ruffians made of that
miserable hour, and of the hour and a half

before it. In the first place, they never
came to their lesson; she had to seek them
all over the garden. When found, and told
to come, August would say, " De suite,
madame ;" Carl would answer nothing ; but
each would go on with his occupation, exactly as if she had not spoken. Nora would
wait a few minutes, and then ask them if
they were coming ? Carl would answer,
" Que c'était un ennui, pardie, que ces
sacrés leçons d'Anglais !" August would
laugh; and they would go on fishing, knock-
ing each other over, playing with the goat,
making dirt pies, eating cherries or peaches,
climbing about the hermitage, or whatever
else might be their business at the moment.
At last, Nora would say that she must go
and tell madame, if they would not come.
August would answer, " Oui, allez, s'il vous
plaît, madame; cela nous donnera du temps !"
but Carl usually swore, and muttered that
she might go " au diable" for what he cared.
Then Nora would call madame to her assistance, and sometimes, in consideration of the
latter's threats, entreaties, and reproaches,

carried on during five or ten minutes, the boys would at last sulkily turn from what they were about, and follow the ladies home. By this time they were, of course, in a delightful temper for learning ; usually, Carl sat and sulked, and swore he would not write or read a word, which threat he would sometimes carry out till within ten minutes of the end of the lesson, when he would become suddenly "sage," lest his papa should be told of his behaviour, and write or read at a great rate. August usually made fun of everything Nora said, or would implore her to give them "une leçon de conversation," which meant that the hour was to be spent in French talk, upon all manner of subjects, with a few words of English here and there.

"Madame Anna" had finally prohibited this style of English study, and was resolute in keeping to the reading, exercises, and dictation with which she had first begun. Not so they: they made the English hour one of true wretchedness to her (and she was wretched enough without that, God knows) : she tried her best, and they tried their worst ; she endeavoured to keep her temper, and they did what they could to irritate it ; she taught as well as— with such pupils, and with no great mental or physical power in herself—she could teach ; they learned the least they could, in the slovenliest possible way. How little they would have contrived to learn during her stay it is impossible to determine ; but, fortunately for their poor instructress, monsieur had decreed that the ordinary evening lesson should be given in the salle-à-manger in his presence ; and the boys were then compelled to behave decently.

As for Fritz, he was always, when once caught, brought to his lessons roaring, " à se faire entendre au village," as his nurse was constantly telling him. When seated in the school-room, he would fling all the books and cahiers from the table, turn over the chairs, kick off his boots and socks one by one, and scream till the wonder was he did not go off into a fit. The only thing to be done was to wait till he was exhausted, or until "un bon mouvement" took place somewhere within him, or until his governess, his mother, and Louise, by dint of alternate threats and promises, had induced him to approach the table, and with a voice hoarser and more rugged than usual, with screaming, commence his reading lesson. On one occasion, when he had been conducting himself in the above style for about a quarter of an hour, " une visite" (it was the first time anyone had called at the house since Nora became resident at St. Pierre) was announced ; and madame hastily gave orders that Fritz should be set free, as such a "tapage" was intolerable. Fritz ceased screaming on the instant, seized his hat, clapped it on his head, and looking with dry eyes, flushed face, and a maliciously triumphant air at his governess, exclaimed, " Ainsi, vous-voyez, madame !" and rushed out to enjoy himself.

Once in every three or four weeks—sometimes oftener—a pale, dark-eyed, bad, and unhealthy-looking boy of about fifteen,

called "Edmond," used to come up to St.
Pierre to spend the afternoon with August
and Carl. This young fellow was up to
every wickedness, and acquainted with every
sort of vice. His whole nature was low and
profligate, yet he was allowed to spend
whole hours—where he liked, how he liked,
and alone—with two children of eleven and
twelve years of age. The two Höffners
were not without some good points; properly trained, in fact, they would have been
fine boys, and under good influence (if
Heaven were yet merciful enough to grant
them any good influence), might still become men of sense, of heart, of honour.
August sometimes showed great natural
kindliness and tenderness of character. It
was seldom, even now, that he grieved his
mother's already sore and aching heart by a
rough or unkind word, or that he refused
her any service—almost brutally thought-
less or reckless as he could be at times
in his treatment of others. Carl, though
addicted to passions and to violences which
baffle description, had the germs in him of a
sort of frankness and courage; but this

boy, this "Edmond," was of the worst
type, of the worst sort of French "Lycéen,"
and the Lord above us knows that there
is nothing much worse, or much lower,
than that upon this earth. Some of the
"bonnes" represented at last to madame—
who knew and seemed to care to know, no
more of Edmond than that he was invariably polite and pleasant towards herself,
and that her sons "s'amusaient" with him
—that they had positive proof of the young
gentleman's being an entirely unfit com-
panion for her, or for any other boys, and
begged that he should be allowed to come
there no more. Madame carried the com-
plaints to monsieur, and monsieur forbade
Edmond the house for three months, after
which time he was allowed to return, under
a promise "d'être sage," which promise, after
having shown himself to be devoid of all
honour, or all shame, he was trusted to keep.

Nora could not help wondering what
sort of places the "Lycées," or high schools,
of French towns were, if this Edmond were
a specimen of the elder pupils, and August

and Carl Höffner specimens, rather above
the average, of the younger ones. From
the accounts they gave her of the deceit, the
disrespect, the disregard, the "moquerie"
with which the masters of the juvenile
classes were treated, she could only imagine that her own task in the way of
teaching was comparatively an enviable
one—the difference being, that she was
treated with open rudeness, incivility, and
inattention during two or three hours in
the week, and that they were treated with
half-concealed and half-repressed incivility,
rudeness, and inattention, and an entire
system of deceit and lying, throughout the
whole of it. She used to try, as well as
she was able, to instil the love of, and the
courage for, truth into the mind of little
Fritz, who, in his better moments, was a
child of great feeling, and very amenable to
good influences.

"Don't tell lies, Fritzkin, when you go
to the Lycée," she would say to him sometimes. "It does no good, and you are
always found out; and *le bon Dieu* won't
love you if you don't speak the truth."

" I'm not going to tell lies' when I go to
the Lycée," little Fritz said to his brothers
one day. " Madame Anna says God won't
love me if I do."

" Won't you though ?" exclaimed Carl,
while August laughed. " You'll soon learn
to tell them. Why, all the boys do."

" But it will be very wicked of you if
you encourage your little brother to do the
same," said Nora, with indignation. " You
should try to help him to be good."

" Oh, let him try," laughed August ; " it
will do no harm. You are very serious this
afternoon, madame !"

After they had left the room, little Fritz
put his arms round his governess's neck,
kissed her, and said, in his hoarse, rugged
voice—

" Never mind, Madame Anna ! I will
be a good boy all the same, and not tell
lies. N'ayez-pas peur !"

She caught the little fellow suddenly to
her breast, and burst into a passionate fit
of crying.

" Don't cry, madame," said Fritzkin. " Is
it because you want to see your mother

again, that you cry? Mademoiselle Isabelle used to cry for that, and she's gone to see her mother now. I would go back for a few days to England, if I were you, and see your mother."

Troublesome and totally undisciplined as these two children, Fritz and Hilda, were, Nora used sometimes to think that the life at St. Pierre, both for their mother, Louise, and herself, would have been intolerably dull without them. They were, at least, a continual occupation; and when they were "sages," their intelligent interest in everything that was told them, and their appreciation of the slightest effort that was made to amuse, or even to instruct, them, was something refreshing.

With Hilda, however, any attempt at moral improvement was not so successful as it was with Fritz. She had more cunning, more "esprit de moquerie," and far less openness of disposition than her brother. To her the advantages of truth, as opposed to indiscriminate story-telling, were yet unknown and incomprehensible;

besides, she preferred story-telling. Fritz, on the contrary, had improved considerably in the art of rendering a faithful account of himself and his proceedings, during the time, Louise said, of Mademoiselle Isabelle's residence, and now only required "keeping up to it." Hilda had been found almost impossible to influence. She was very imaginative, and full of "méchanceté," hardihood, and resolution. She was a little savage to her nurses, and she had no particular fondness for the English governess.

One day, after she had been screaming fearfully for some time, because she had "mal aux oreilles," Nora, who had stood by her till she was fit to drop, said—

"But, ma bonne chérie, no one will believe you have ear-ache if you scream so dreadfully. When any one has ear-ache, le bruit fait mal. Ne sais-tu pas ça ?"

"Oh oui," replied this little thing of four years, in a voice and with an expression of supreme contempt. "Vous n'y entendez rien, parce que vous êtes Anglaise ! Les Anglaises n'ont jamais mal aux oreilles !"

CHAPTER XIII.

A SISTER of Louise's French governess—by name Mademoiselle Agnès Thérèse Picard —was engaged as musical teacher to Louise, August, and Carl, and used to come to St. Pierre twice in the week, to give them what was termed by compliment their "leçons de piano." As Louise seldom, and the boys never, practised for her, and as Carl invariably behaved with the utmost inattention and rudeness during the greater part of his lesson (indeed, with a species of brutality during the whole of it, if he happened to be in a bad humour), the poor lady's task was none of the pleasantest. She tried, in succession, coaxing, scolding, and flattering, without avail. It was "Maintenant, mon petit Carl, jouez donc ! Tâchez donc de me plaire, mon petit Carl ! Voyons, cher enfant, ne voulez-vous pas que je dise à ton père comme tu fais des progrès ?" and so on, *ad infinitum.* The pieces and exercises were brought up in exactly the same state of imperfection one week as they had been the last.

It happened one day that M. Höffner stayed at home to nurse a cold ; his way of nursing a cold, or any other ailment, being to sit in the *salle-à-manger* all day, with a fur cap on his head, a long dressing-gown enveloping his figure, speaking to no one, reading the newspapers, and drinking pints of " tisane." In the evening he asked his children to play to him, by way of a little enlivenment. He said nothing while the bungling performances lasted, but went on reading, and puffing at his pipe. When Carl, however, looking very foolish, rose from the piano, M. Höffner turned to his wife, and after roundly abusing her for the manner in which his children played, said that, as he did not choose to pay money for

nothing, and as he plainly saw that the
children did not practise from one month's
end to another, she might dismiss " Mademoiselle 'Chose' sur le champ." Did she
come to-morrow ? Yes, she did come to-
morrow. Well, then, she might go as soon
as she came ; he would have no more of
her ; and in the meantime, where was the
key of the piano? In the instrument? Good!
Then no one should play on it for the future,
except Madame Anna, who might ask madame for the key when she wanted it, or
madame herself. Monsieur then rose,
locked the piano, hung the key by the side
of a score of others inside the door of his
wife's linen closet, and re-seated himself
to his pipe and his book. There was
absolute silence in the room as long as
he stayed, and he stayed about half an
hour. Then he got up and went to bed.
As soon as he was well out of the room,
Louise was seized with a veritable "accès
de folie." She wept, she gesticulated, she
paced the room, she declared she would
throw herself to the swans, that " le piano

était un étude détestable ;" and finally, that she did not wish to live.

" Mais calme toi donc ; calme toi," her mother kept reiterating ; " ne t'excite pas tant !"; and at last she gave her some eau sucrée and sent her to bed. Nora thought that the young lady had got, on the whole, less than she deserved for her idleness ; but Louise's feeling was, and continued to be, that she was a frightfully injured individual, and that her papa's " humeurs " were the curse of the household. It was indubitable that they were ; but indubitable also, that there existed, now and then, cause for them.

The morning following " ce fracas à cause du piano," and the day devoted to tisane and his dressing-gown, on the part of Monsieur, that gentleman was sufficiently restored to go about the house in his usual habiliments, but did not purpose going to town until the afternoon. The whole household had reason to be thankful, whenever monsieur (not being in a bad temper) thought fit to remain for a few extra hours .

"chez-soi." On these occasions Fritz and
Hilda, who were equally possessed of tem-
pers apparently got first hand from the
very Father of Evil himself, and who were
allowed—in company with their brother
Carl—to give way to the insanest passions
for which any shadow of an excuse could
be "made or created," and to the fullest
extent of which flesh and blood are capable
—(Hilda being, in fact, as thorough a little
"diablesse" as ever yet existed in France
or out of it)—these two, we say, were compelled to behave with something like
decency, and their "bonne" had a short
respite from misery, from cuffs and from
"injures."

The sufferers, be it said here, from the
uncommon disposition of the young Höffners were five in number; firstly, their
mother, whose too sweet and gentle nature
stood shocks from their and her husband's
"accès de colère" combined, enough to send
any ordinary woman insane ; secondly, the
English governess, whoever she might
happen to be ; thirdly, the unhappy bonne

d'enfants, whose life was a foretaste (let us hope she was never destined to have a further one) of the infernal regions themselves; fourthly, the musical teacher (whether she were French or English) ; and fifthly, the "femme de chambre," who once averred that it required "un garçon de chambre" to stand the usage she received from one and the other, and that monsieur would do well to advertise for such a domestic.

On the morning of which we write, however, quiet prevailed within the precints of St. Pierre. It was an ominous calm. Everyone knew what was coming, when monsieur asked his wife for the key of her especial "grenier," and marched up the stairs—followed by Fitz and Hilda, in high, but repressed glee— and straight into that hallowed chamber. His next business was to open all the cupboards, ransack them, and make a heap on the floor of everything which he considered rubbish, without the slightest reference to what madame's own views concerning the items might be. The game was then (for it appeared that these rummages, with their subsequent committal of effects to the flames, occurred at perio-dical intervals), for the young ones to assist their father in carrying out the spoil to some convenient place in the garden, monsieur then setting fire to the mass, and Fritz and Hilda dancing around the conflagration with frantic gesticulations and shrieks of joy.

There was something in the whole thing which made Nora's heart tremble. She had felt ever since the first week of her installation at St. Pierre as if she stood on a volcano, and now and then the ground seemed to shake and rumble ominously beneath her feet. The sight of that fire, of the flushed, hard face of the master (her master), as he stood looking on, and the shouting and dancing of those two imps, turned her sick. Having no other hope or prospect left her on earth, no means of gain-ing her daily bread except by leading, for what years were left to her, some such life as the one she was leading now, the poor girl was striving hard to fulfil the duties of her strange position, and like any other servant knew that her future must hang on the " character" she would obtain if she left, or if she were turned away. She had tried to forget—to force back into a dark corner of her memory, on which she would fain have turned the key—all the brilliance, the guilt, the folly of her last three or four years ; she had tried to think of herself as a girl once more, when she taught her little sisters, and was innocent ; she dressed, moved, spoke quietly and plainly ; she worked with what strength and knowledge she had ; she used to read a little out of Louise's French Testament every night, and she tried to pray. She endeavoured not to think of the man she had loved, and who had been her ruin, and she hoped that God would befriend her, and keep her from destitution and disgrace.

Nora had never been, and never could be, an earnest, a noble, or a deeply-feeling woman, that was impossible, but she was not bad ; and she was gaining in her trying life, more principle, more humility, and more steadiness of purpose, than she had ever possessed yet.

She was going into her bed-room on the day of which we write—the sight of that fire having made her feel ill and faint—when, in passing through the night-nursery, she saw Madame Höffner, Louise, and the bonne d'enfants all looking out of the window, from which they could see the fire. Madame retired on the governess's entrance, the others, however, continued to peer out, and then duck their heads hastily if monsieur turned his face in that direction.

" Look here, Madame Anna," exclaimed Louise, in high glee ; " I managed to get hold of this—and this—and this, before they were put in," and she showed several beautiful pieces of silk and satin ; " but isn't it a pity ? Mamma saw her wedding slippers burnt, and she wanted always to keep them ! I wouldn't keep them," she added nonchalantly, " if I had married such a man as papa, allez ! No danger that I will marry a German ; if I do not have a Frenchman, I will have nobody. But look—look, madame! they are throwing on straw and wood to keep up the fire! Ah! it was only for a minute, to please Fritz and Hilda. They are sorry it is over."

Nora stood at the window for a minute or two, and then went on into her room. When Louise ran into the garden to meet her little brother and sister, the bonne made an excuse to come to Madame Anna, and leaning against the doorway, said—

"Est-ce merveilleux, madame, that those children have no heart? Why did not monsieur give away those things instead of burning them? Moi, je trouve que c'est une horreur que ces feux-de-joie; on ne sait jamais ce qu'on perd. J'aurais pu faire des cadeaux, à toute ma famille des effets qu'il a brulés!" And then, hearing herself called, she hurried away to get her children "arrangés" for déjeûner.

It was probably in consequence of seeing so many valuable "effets" uselessly dis-posed of, that the bonne in question—by name Valentine—conceived the idea of appropriating a few miscellaneous articles belonging to the family to her own use, or at any rate of securing them within her own "armoire," where, by some accident, they were discovered by madame. Nora had been with Mdlle. Höffner to her "cours," and the two were approaching the house on their return, when Fritz and Hilda rushed out on to the verandah, screaming at the top of their voices,

"Valentine est une voleuse ; et elle s'en va !"

"Valentine a thief!" repeated Madame Anna, turning rather pale (with the children's words had come the sensation of that far off rumbling again beneath her feet) ; "what has she taken ?"

"She has taken deux mouchoirs de Louise, and a collar, and a thimble," shrieked Fritz.

"And some tape and some chiffons de soie," added Hilda. And then both the children turned round and scampered up the stone staircase, Fritz's large-nailed boots (he wore week in and week out, a pair rather too small for Carl, but too heavy for August) making an infernal clatter upon the stone steps and the uncarpeted floors as he went. Nora went up to the poor nurse-maid, who was sobbing her heart out, over her box, as she packed it ready for her departure. Her aunt, she said, to whom she must now go, would "die of grief" when she heard why she had been sent away. She was to be ready for the next omnibus ; it would be here in five minutes, she said. . . . . "Adieu, Madame Anna ; adieu, Fritz ; . . . adieu, ma petite Anna." Then more sobs ; then round came the omnibus; and then the little "voleuse" was gone.

"I am very, very sorry for the poor girl," said madame, as she watched her departure from out of the dining-room windows, "but my husband would have been too angry if I had kept her. You see when girls do this kind of thing once, they will do it again ; it is the way with all of them !"

In the afternoon came up Mdlle. Agnès Thérèse, who had been reinstated as Louise's

musical teacher, Nora having now the agré-
ment of teaching the young gentlemen ; and
she it was who had had the infelicity to
recommend Valentine, some two months
previously. (There were on an average two
changes of "bonnes" in every six weeks at
St. Pierre.)

"What is this I hear?" exclaimed Mdlle.
Thérèse, entering the salle-à-manger, like a
true tragedy queen ; "I implore—I conjure
you, madame, to tell me this is not true !
. . . . Ah, mon Dieu !" she continued, when
she had heard part of the story ; "à vous
dire, madame, que sa tante m'avait dit que la
fille était tout-à-fait sans vices !—qu'elle ne
lui connaissait pas un défaut !—Madame, you
might have sent her to prison, with chains
about her neck, but you have such infinite
goodness ! . . 'A vous dire mon déséspoir,
madame ! C'est tout de ma faute !" and so
on for half an hour, as pauses in the hideous
recital gave mademoiselle opportunity for
her expressions of grief and indignation.
Hilda happening to enter the room with her
doll, mademoiselle first looked at, and then

turned from her, with an air of faintness, as if the sight of such sweet innocence were too much for her, and murmured " Pauvre bijou ! pauvre ange ! To think she has had such a serpent about her ! Why, chère madame, you may be thankful she has not robbed you of all !—has not poisoned anybody !—has not murdered anybody !—Oh, mon Dieu !—la malheureuse—la misérable —la méchante !"

There could scarcely have been more disturbance made in the house, more consternation and horror expressed, if the unfortunate " bonne" had been discovered in the act of putting venomous snakes into the children's beds, or poisoning their morning's " soupe aux choux."

The English teacher went upstairs after Mdlle. Thérèse's departure, locked herself into her room, and after pacing it restlessly for some time, suddenly dropped upon her knees.

" Oh, my God !" she said, " oh, merciful God, have pity on me !" It was all she said, and all she could say ; and she re-

peated the words till they lost all meaning
for her. " I am far worse than that poor
girl," she groaned, when at last she flung
herself on her bed, her face hidden in her
hands ; " I am the real malheureuse—misérable, méchante ! It is I they would send
to prison ' with chains,' if they could do it
—and if they knew what I am. What is
to become of me, if they send me away ?"
. . . . And then, as the excitement and
distress, almost the terror of her heart increased—for she was weak and unfitted for
endurance—she sobbed out, " Oh, Rochefort ! why did I ever leave you ? Oh, to
be in his arms once more, safe—safe—safe !
Oh, what have I left ? What have I found
instead ?"

*   *   *   *

CHAPTER XIV.

M. Höffner's establishment, though surrounded by country houses in which people led more or less gay, or cheerful, or varied lives, was conducted on a plan of his own, which, to use a mild term, may be designated as "conventual." No one was ever allowed inside the gates except the laundress who came to fetch and to bring the clothes, and the gardener, whose home was in the nearest suburb of the town. The bread, the groceries, the meat (when it could be got in), and the milk, were passed through the "guichet" in the garden door; there was only a caller about twice a year, and madame went to X—— about as often as she mustered up spirits to go to church (otherwise "au temple "), which event occurred about once in a month.

Madame Höffner, who seemed to feel much the monotony and isolation of her life, told Nora once that "there was no country on earth where you could be so frightfully dull, or so insanely gay, as in France. There was," she said, "none of the free, social, hospitable intercourse of families, and of young people, that there was in Germany and in England." As a rule (en province, at least), ladies lived the life of recluses—of simple "femmes de ménage," or of simple "femmes de société," which latter term did not always mean everything that was most innocent or edifying. The laws of betrothal and marriage in France governed all other laws, and they governed them to the destruction of all healthy freedom, all happiness and sociability in the relation of families with one another. Madame felt strongly, and used to express herself strongly, on these points. She was a woman who had been made timid by circumstances, but her character was full of intelligence, of power, of sympathy, and of real kindliness and frankness. Poor Nora clung to and loved her, as she had never clung to or loved a woman before ; and sometimes, in her present desolate and friendless condition, felt an indescribable dread at the idea of being separated from her.

"But I think," madame would say, with a sigh, "that I have been particularly unfortunate, so I ought not to judge. Of course, it is very rare that a woman in my position leads a life so entirely isolated as mine ; at least, it is very rare in X——. I had always heard there was so much 'life' here ; but it has not been my experience." At other times, madame would say, " I have a great deal to be thankful for, after all. You see, there are my children"—these poor French ladies have one or two each ; three is a large family, four enormous ! And again, my husband, whatever may be his faults, is faithful to me, and never leaves me for an evening alone. I know ladies in X——, and in Y——, whose husbands leave them night after night for the gaming-table, for gaming is the regular recreation of the French gentlemen in these large towns ; M. Höffner never plays anything but a game of billiards with his partner, or his nephews."

These "games of billiards" used to come off every "Dimanche" after dinner ; "Dimanche" being the only day in the week when any influx from the outer world penetrated the well-guarded enclosure of St. Pierre. Then, monsieur, who always went to town for an hour or two in the morning, used to bring up with him to dinner, at three o'clock, his bachelor friend and partner, M. Brunet, his nephew, and a French "capitaine." It was, therefore, a red-letter day at St. Pierre. When surrounded by his friends, monsieur conversed like an ordinary, and even a pleasant being, instead of scolding like a madman ; was agreeable to his guests, and did not rail against all men and women as if they were profligates, Jesuits, idiots, or thieves. It was his custom on ordinary days, on the slightest, or on no provocation, to begin his tirades against the world in general about the time the meat was put on the table. He took his soup in silence, and it was not until after it was removed that any one could tell in what sort of a humour he had sat down to it. When he began the process of carving, by turning to Hilda, who sat on his right hand, and saying, in German, " Well, my child, and what hast thou been doing all day ?" everyone began to sit at ease ; if he worked his carving-knife and fork rapidly, and looked neither to the right hand nor to the left, things looked bad, and no one stirred or spoke. Sometimes his humour showed itself as soon as he entered the hall door. It was usual for almost every member of the household to retire to the upper regions about a quarter of an hour before the usual time for monsieur's and the boys' return, and to collect evidence, by either eye or ear (generally it was by ear), of the sort of temper in which the head of the family came home, before venturing downstairs. As soon as a scene began, Fritz would be heard stamping up the nursery stairs in his hob-nailed boots, vociferating in a horse whisper, " Hilda, Hilda ! viens donc entendre papa, *qui crie !*" The two children then, in high excitement, their eyes sparkling with glee, would hang together over the banisters, their *bonne* sometimes standing a step or two above ; and possibly " Madame Anna" on the landing above that, white and trembling, and straining her ears to catch the words that were roared forth below, in a fury that seemed at times absolutely inhuman.

On one occasion, when dinner had been delayed a quarter of an hour, in order that madame and the unfortunate " femme de chambre" might have their duty in relation to certain stains upon the marble pavement of the hall pointed out to them, the family were assembled at last round the table, sitting on the proverbial " pins and needles," and silently expectant of their " potage." The potage was served round without a word by the flushed and trembling waitress, who seemed hardly capable of holding the plates. The " bouilli " then followed, and was carved with awful and ominous rapidity; but that also was handed round and eaten without any contretemps occurring. Then came a dish of "asperges," the sugar, vinegar, and oil to make the sauce for which were carried round in due form to monsieur.

"What's this?" struck forth the master, in a tone that made everyone's heart leap into his or her mouth.

"Isn't it sugar, Wilhelm?" asked madame. "What is the matter with it?"

"Sugar!" roared Höffner, swearing 'à faire dresser les cheveux sur la tête,' "is it a new form of your confounded idleness to mix brown and white sugar together? Take the dish away;" and he pushed sugar basin, dish, oil and vinegar cruets into the middle of the table, and signed to the bonne to remove the lot. Every stick of that asparagus was taken into the kitchen, and it was a splendid dish-full, and there was no other vegetable for dinner, and no "plat sucré." Dinner being, therefore, finished, there was nothing to prevent monsieur from haranguing at leisure on the way in which his household was conducted; and he probably did it all the better, that he had just deprived himself of half, and the best half, of his meal. A little noise being made by the terrified bonne in putting the dishes through the "passe-plat" of the office, monsieur proceeded to introduce into his harangue (as usual upon such occasions), and with fiery glances towards madame, a certain "paysan" (Heaven alone knew where this man lived, what were his antecedents, or what the occupations of himself and family), who, however, resided in an immaculately conducted cottage, where nothing was ever broken, or out of order — no "tapage" ever made indoors or out while he took his meals, and whose wife had every good and housewifely quality which a woman can possess. This "paysan"—he was called at St. Pierre, " le paysan de monsieur," as we talk of "Macaulay's school-boy"—was always dragged, head and neck, and without a moment's warning, into monsieur's discourse, whenever he was nearly mad. The assembled family were presented to him evening after evening, whenever there was any contretemps before, during, or after dinner, and his establishment grew more and more perfect, his kitchen tidier and tidier, till it was a matter of wondering conjecture to some of his hearers what would be the comforts the "peasant" would ultimately have around him, when he should appear for the last time. M. Höffner's own house, it appeared, was always in the position of a "Schweinstall" or "écurie de cochons;" and though madame, the bonnes, and the English governess, seemed, one or other, to be tidying from morning till night, they were kept informed that their united efforts produced nothing but "des cochonneries," in comparison with the exquisite neatness and comfort achieved by the peasant's wife.

It should be noted, however, that besides the "paysan" there existed somewhere or other a certain "cabaret," where there was not during the entire day, as much noise as in M. Höffner's kitchen while dinner was being served. This cabaret Höffner used to describe as if he had seen it.

It used to amaze Nora — as indeed it
amazed everyone—to see with what gentle
calm and humility poor madame took all
her husband's raving. She never replied
to him and never defended herself; and
though it was currently reported and believed that she suffered much, and wept
often and long, in her own room, she never
shed a tear, or seemed more than quietly
depressed and sad, when in the presence of
others. Her affection for, and belief in
him, remained through everything so tender
and true (Nora used to wonder—before she
became aware of this—if it was for the
sake of the children, that she did not run
away and beg her bread, rather than live
with him), that she would often say in
excuse for his temper, " after all he is right
when he scolds about things ! He perhaps
expresses himself a little strongly, but you
see, Madame Anna, his mother was such a
perfect housekeeper ! She had such man-
agement, such power with her servants ;
she directed her household with such a
strong hand—that no wonder he finds me

very deficient." Nora never knew whether madame herself had been acquainted with this extraordinary lady, or whether she took her "on faith" from her husband; in which latter case it might be supposed that some of her perfections were imaginary, like those with which the fertility of monsieur's brain furnished "la femme du paysan," or the "dame du cabaret."

On Sundays, however, there was, as we have said—superficially at least—"peace on earth and good-will towards men" within the walls of St. Pierre. The mornings were tranquilly spent by the English governess and her eldest pupil in reading, Louise generally bringing her book into Nora's room, that she might have the benefit of her table, ottoman, or easy-chair—the rooms in this house being all comfortably, and many of them very handsomely and richly furnished — and also that she might have some one to talk to in the pauses of her story. It may be remarked here, that Louise and her brothers had certain bound volumes of a publication entitled "Magasin

pour les jeunes Personnes," delivered over
for their special perusal, and these books
were kept inside one of the cupboards of
the salle-à-manger, or upstairs in Louise's
bedroom. Nora had now and then taken
one up, and read a story, or part of one, or
turned the leaves to look at the pictures,
of which there were plenty. The histories
were chiefly concerning young men and
their love affairs,—or rather their liaisons.
The very good young men introduced into
these narratives were faithful to their
" fiancées," and had no mistresses ; the
tolerably good ones had first mistresses, and
then, reforming through the influence of
the very good ones, abandoned them, and
married " des jeunes filles," who were
" pures, modestes, pieuses comme des anges !"
—the bad young men became hopelessly
entangled with the ladies of their demi-
monde, and either fell into poverty, or
broke their mothers' hearts, or went out of
their minds, because some " jeune fille "
(again) of angelic character, and almost
unearthly beauty, on whom they had set

their affections, utterly refused to "se marier avec eux," and bestowed her hand on some "cher bon Jean" instead. These stories were intended to be extremely moral and improving; and, taking them in comparison with the greater portion of the entertaining literature published by the French press, they were of course in every respect pure, elevating, ennobling — nay, even severe in their religious principle and moral teaching. As Louise usually read in one of these books for an hour every night, after going to bed, it is to be hoped they produced this effect upon her.

After some time spent in reading, the task of dressing for dinner commenced. On week-days this operation was conducted in a short space of time, and the quarter of an hour devoted to it by the various members of the household was overshadowed by fear of what might be coming. It was not pleasant to reflect that the mistress might be told, as she sat at the head of her table, that she kept her house like a sty; that her husband might be accommodated and

served like a pig for all she cared :—to be
asked if she wasn't ashamed of her "sacré"
idleness, negligence, and slovenliness ?—to
be sworn at before her daughters, shamed
before her sons, and then not spoken to
for the rest of the evening ? " Sacr-r-ré
nom de Dieu !" or " Sacr-r-ré diable !"—
brought out with a grin, and a hiss, and
a glare of two light eyes, and accompanied
by torrents of abuse, are not expletives
calculated to assist the digestion of the
person to whom they are addressed, or, in
fact, to be pleasant adjuncts to anybody's
dinner. It had happened upon occasions
that little Fritz began swearing at dinner
in imitation of his father. Höffner would
then turn pale, and stop him at the beginning of his " Sacré's," with a sudden
" Sacré papier ! sacré pelote ! c'est ça ce
que tu veux dire, n'est-ce pas ?" with a
look which told master Fritz he had better
mean that, and nothing else, in his father's
presence. At such moments Nora would
be almost sorry for the man, and wondered
if there were ever times when he wished he

had treated his poor wife better during their fifteen years of married life.

He generally made her presents after scolding her, and would speak to, or of her in terms of affection ; he was devoted to her if she were ill, and he was unhappy when she was away. Moreover, he was not uncharitable, was not ungenerous in his way ; he had a sort of reverence for the Name he was for ever blaspheming, and folded his hands with his children over their grace at meals, saying sternly and gravely, " Ordentlich, mein kind. Say that again slowly and beziemlich !" if the few words of prayer were not reverently and distinctly uttered.

On the blessed " first day of the week," everybody at St. Pierre could dress themselves, and try to look their neatest, and prettiest, without the fear of impending trouble and catastrophe. The dinners were always good, the master always agreeable and in good humour, and the conversation always interesting. One day a certain M. Décrand from M—— joined the party in place of "M. le Capitaine," who was not well; and M. Brunet was also absent, it being the fête-day of his brother's wife. Décrand was a little, intelligent-looking, dark-eyed man, with a rapid and decided way of talking; and the conversation, before the meat course was half through, naturally turned upon politics. "The next revolution" was talked of, as one might talk of the next Derby. "It will come in five years at the latest, probably sooner," said Décrand calmly, as he helped himself to gravy; "France cannot exist without revolutions."

"But you are a Bonapartist, monsieur, n'est-ce pas?" inquired M. Ferdinand Höffner, looking across the table at the speaker.

"Yes, I am a Bonapartist," replied Décrand, "because I believe the French must be governed with a strong hand—wise, if possible, but always strong. We have as much liberty now as we can manage. I have too much, for my part. The nation cannot rule itself. It is humiliating to have to say so, but it is true. We have not much to complain of in the Emperor's administration, and he has done a great deal for us. I don't say if we were English or Germans we shouldn't have a lot to complain of; but we are not English or Germans. If we have a revolution, neither side will gain anything,and both will lose much."

"You have a high opinion, monsieur, of the national character," remarked Höffner, glancing at him and laughing. Höffner hated the French in theory, and in practice made two Frenchmen his greatest friends.

"There is no national character, properly speaking," returned M. Décrand. " There are clever and thoughtful men here and there ; but for the most part, we have all the same faults, in greater or less degree—ridiculous vanity, bombast, love of theatrical attitude in all we do, and say, and print, fickleness, and love of agitation and change ⁺ɔ a horrible extent ! I tell you," he went on, his face flushing as he spoke, "the French blood is impregnated with the Reign of Terror. Our grandfathers and grandmothers sucked in that poison with their mother's milk. We are all born with a thirst for agitation, for excitement, almost for blood. We shall never be a nation like another till that dies out of us."

"Or till we can be united in one great aim," observed M. Ferdinand, in a suggestive sort of way.

"We can never be united," replied the Frenchman quickly. "There are those who are always talking about liberty, and those who know what all that nonsense means—two great classes for you at once (though one is much larger than the other), and two utterly irreconcilable classes. The agitators, of course, are the last to know how to use the freedom they are always yelling about. They have more now than they can rein in; many of them are intoxicated already on their saddles, and 'perdent les têtes.'"

Höffner took up the wine-bottle, and poured some into everybody's glass. When he had done so, he remarked—

"In spite of all your Emperor's good qualities, Décrand, I believe that if one single editor of a Parisian journal had the courage to write against him and his government, at the end of fifteen days Napoleon would be driven from the Tuileries."

"Not yet," returned Décrand coolly; "the time isn't ripe for it. The journal would be simply suppressed, and the editor imprisoned, and we should hear no more of it. The Reds will not get the upper hand yet."

"But the Reds are always there," answered Höffner, laughing, "and never will be sat upon, beyond a certain time. They keep rising to the surface, as offal rises to the surface of water."

"Yes," returned the Bonapartist, "and if they keep rising, it will come to this, that the next revolution will be that of the rich against the poor; the next Reign of Terror that in which the aristocracy and the merchants, and all men who wish for peace and quietude, will drive tumbrils full of these insane wretches through the streets, to a second 'Place de la Guillotine'!"

The next Sunday, Höffner said, laughing,

to his friend " M. le Capitaine," who was
again seated in his right place at madame's
left side—

" It is a good thing you were not here
last Sunday, mon Capitaine, pour entendre
Décrand. If you had been, there would
probably have been a passage of arms."

M. le Capitaine, however, who had just
helped himself to some very excellent " gâ-
teau de foie de volaille " and a good glass of
wine, was disposed to feel graciously towards
all men, and only said, shrugging his shoulders, " Ah, well, people must have their
opinions ;" and he soon turned the talk on
Algeria, of which ground he was acknowledged master, amusing everybody by his
anecdotes, and entertaining them with his
reminiscences. M. le Capitaine was not
always quite correct in his information as to
foreign countries, and the habits and customs of their inhabitants ; but it is to be
presumed he was invariably correct when
he gave information respecting Egypt and
Algeria. He once observed to the assembled
party at dinner, " that although they grew

so much tea in China, none of the natives
ever drank any ;" and M. Höffner replied,
" Is that possible ?   I did not know it.
Mon Dieu, que c'est drôle, ça !"

Sometimes the captain (it might be by
way of compliment to one of the loveliest
Englishwomen he had ever seen) turned the
talk upon the Crimea, and the bravery of
the English.

" Their bravery and their perseverance,"
he would say, addressing Höffner, " were
sans pareille—mais sans pareille !   At an
attack on one of the forts, I saw our men
precipitate themselves with an extreme
ardour, and I saw them repulsed.   The
English, who marched slowly, and almost
as if they were going to a funeral, threw
themselves with an irresistible force against
the enemy, and were successful."

M. le Capitaine helped himself to wine,
and cast a momentary glance at the English governess.   She looked very much
flushed, but she was not smiling ; he could
not tell whether she were pleased or not.
(N.B.—As it is not the custom in France for

gentlemen ever to speak to "institutrices,"
or for the "institutrices" ever to speak
to gentlemen, those ladies engaged in
tuition who have the least fancy for flirt-
ing, or for general conversation in company,
had better keep to their native lands.)

"You ought to tell us something now
on the side of the French soldiers, monsieur," said August, "I know they are
brave, too."

"Brave !" echoed the captain, colouring
all over his bronzed face, "they are so brave,
August, that they do not need my praise.
Find me a Frenchman who does not think
the French army brave. But I can tell
you something else of them, my boy—they
can cook. How do the English soldiers do
their cooking when they are on the march ?
If they are without their cooks, they have no
notion what to do for themselves ; but when
I have been marching, I have seen a few
dozen of our soldiers run on before, dig
some holes, light the bits of wood and stick
they have picked up by the roadside as they
came along, and in a few minutes we all have
fire, coffee, or soup !"

"I will be a French soldier," said little Fritz, as he spooned his mutton and fried potatoes into his mouth, "je n'aimerais pas, pas dîner, moi!"

The Sunday after this was a memorable one at St. Pierre. There was a splendid dish of partridges "à la Catalane" on the table at dinner. Höffner, who was in high good humour, and talking all the time, cut them up, and when ready, and neatly distributed on the dish, gave them to the waitress to carry round. She took the dish on her white napkin, commenced her course carefully towards madame, and had nearly reached her, when the dish suddenly slipped —it looked as if it was shot by some invisible power—from her hands, broke, and all the partridges, with their gravy, were on the floor.

It was awful. The face of M. le Capitaine fell in one instant from an expression of jocund expectation to one of blank dismay. He became white, then almost blue; his voice was no more heard; he drank half a

tumbler full of wine and water, for he felt
faint. M. Brunet leaned back in his chair,
and fingered his watch-chain; madame and
the children all looked in one direction.
In that one direction there was perfect
calm; monsieur remained with his hands,
folded together on the tablecloth; he gave
one glance towards the spot where the unhappy bonne knelt, spooning up the dis-
membered partridges and their delicious
sauce; then he unclasped his hands, folded
them another way, and said, " Enfin—
c'est fini. What else have you to give us,
frau ?"

" Stewed beef, with carrots," returned
madame, in a voice scarcely audible.

" Let us eat that, then," continued monsieur. " Leave all that saleté on the floor"
(this to the bonne), "and bring us the beef.
That can all be wiped up afterwards."

The floor was so exquisitely clean and
polished, that perhaps none of the party
would have objected to eating the partridges (without the sauce), even now; but
this was not monsieur's idea. If he ever

sent away a "plat" from table, it was never supposed to be heard, thought of, or seen again. It is to be hoped that the servants regaled themselves thereon. On one occa-sion a sucking-pig (the talk and thought of the children for weeks before, and sent from a country inn and farmhouse twelve miles off), was brought to table, half-boiled in-stead of wholly roasted. Once a huge fish, which had been sent up from X—— in ice, and by a special messenger, appeared before the company half-raw, and was sent out quicker than it came in : but never was a morsel of either pig or fish seen again, in any form or shape whatsoever. Monsieur's temper, be it said, stood each of these shocks, as it stood the downfall of the "perdrix," with a stoic imperturbability that was a moral lesson in itself to behold. His hu-mour, however, was diabolical for three days after each event. It was "volcanic" for six days after the partridges. On the seventh it "éclata."

Nora was up in her bedroom, writing to her sister, and waiting for the tea-bell to ring. She had long ago left off hearing from Ernest ; but, in order that she might still appear to have letters from "her husband," her father had consented to direct a number of envelopes, in one of which Miss Heaton enclosed a fortnightly missive from herself or her mother; sometimes only a note in large hand, written by one of the little sisters, who wondered why "Nora stayed so long away," and the youngest of whom would write, "I hope you are coming home soon. I thought you were going to live at Riverswood when you were married. I am getting on with my music, and I have got a new frock for best ; and we are going to a party at Mrs. Robinson's next Tuesday," &c., &c.

She was writing to Lizzy, and was trying not to cry over her letter, when she was startled by the sound of Höffner's voice downstairs, and the violent sobbing of one of the maids. The master was raving and swearing, as if he had gone mad ; and Nora, throwing down her pen, went to the top of the stairs and leaned over the banis-

ters ; her heart beating—as it always did
when she did not know the cause of Monsieur's rage—almost as if it would burst.
She had not long to wait : the poor femme
de chambre—she of the partridges—was
seen coming up the stairs, gasping—weeping—scarcely able to walk, and followed by
the cuisinière, who was also crying, and
looked as scared as if she had just seen a
murder. When Nora could collect anything
like a statement of facts from the two weeping and terrified women—she had followed
them into their room, where one sat holding
her hands to her side, and the other leaned
against the doorway—she found that M.
August and M. Jules had been amusing
themselves, while their elders played billiards, in behaving with brutal rudeness to
the servants ; that Juliette, having borne a
considerable amount of this usage for some
time, suddenly made up her mind she would
bear it no more, and went to madame "pour
lui donner sa huitaine " (to give her notice).
The poor girl had given it once before, but
had then asked to stop ; "and I think,"

she said, "I was mad to do so, Madame
Anna; but I did it for Madame's sake, who
has troubles in her house, de quoi devenir
folle, as you know. And Monsieur came
and raved at me, and called me ' p——e '
(the English translation is a stronger word
than we care to write), and kicked me as I
came up the stairs—yes, kicked me, madame!
—and I am to pack up my things, and go
away when the carriage comes for ' ces
messieurs.' "

" Did he—did he call you that name,
only because you wished to go ?" asked the
English governess, who was as white as a
sheet, and trembling violently.

" No madame," said the cuisinière, showing an unopened letter, which she held in
her hand ; " Juiliette promised to take care
of any letters which might come for Fran-
cine—who left a month ago, you know—
and this came for her, and it's in a man's
handwriting. And M. August saw it, and
told his papa of it, and Monsieur said
Juliette had letters from men, and that she
was ' une mauvaise fille.' "

"Et je suis pauvre, mais je suis honnête !" exclaimed poor Juliette, flashing up through her tears ; "I would not be what Monsieur called me to save myself from starving. Mon Dieu, non ! j'aimerais mieux être morte, avec ma pauvre mère !" And then she began to pack her box ready for going.

When Nora went downstairs to tea, about an hour afterwards ; Monsieur was talking away on general topics to the Captain, and M. Ferdinand was playing with Hilda. Madame did not look discomposed, and was giving out the tea from her little spirit-urn. M. Brunet was not there. At the beginning of the fracas he had walked up to the peg in the vestibule from which depended his hat, taken it therefrom, and made a slight bow to Madame.

"Will you not stay to tea, monsieur?" Madame had demanded.

"Non, merci madame ! je m'en fuis au contraire," returned the bachelor partner ; and he went home immediately, on foot and in the dark.

Nora saw the boys, when they went up

19—2

to bed, imitating in dumb show the kicks
of their papa, and the weeping and gasping
of the poor bonne.   August acted the part
of the master, Carl that of the servant,
and the play was strikingly performed, and
to the life.

"Diable ! mais c'était drôle, n'est-ce pas ?'
she heard one say to the other, as they
tumbled over each other into their bed-
room, struggling to repress their laughter.

END OF VOL. II.

BILLING AND SONS, PRINTERS, GUILDFORD, SURREY.